"I love you, Tanner," she said impulsively.

He smiled. "I know you do."

"How could you know I love you? I've only been here two days, and I've slept upstairs, out of reach."

"Love is more than just sex. You stayed with me, I don't think you're all the way committed to me yet, but you're considering it. You're a little afraid. I believe you think of yourself as a sacrificial maiden being coaxed to fling herself into an active volcano."

"An active volcano?" She considered the comparison. "That's really very close."

"And I've never known anyone who kissed in such an abandoned, committed way. You do some interesting things to me."

"Do you feel this amazing pull between us, too? I get in the same room with you and it's almost frightening."

"Don't be afraid of me, Laura," he said quietly.

"I bet you say that to all the sacrificial maidens."

Dear Reader,

Welcome to Silhouette! Our goal is to give you hours of unbeatable reading pleasure, and we hope you'll enjoy each month's six new Silhouette Desires. These sensual, provocative love stories are both believable and compelling—sometimes they're poignant, sometimes humorous, but always enjoyable.

Indulge yourself. Experience all the passion and excitement of falling in love along with our heroine as she meets the irresistible man of her dreams and together they overcome all obstacles in the path to a happy ending.

If this is your first Desire, I hope it'll be the first of many. If you're already a Silhouette Desire reader, thanks for your support! Look for some of your favorite authors in the coming months: Stephanie James, Diana Palmer, Dixie Browning, Ann Major and Doreen Owens Malek, to name just a few.

Happy reading!

Isabel Swift
Senior Editor

SDRL-7/85

LASS SMALL
To Meet Again

Silhouette Desire
Published by Silhouette Books New York

America's Publisher of Contemporary Romance

SILHOUETTE BOOKS
300 East 42nd St., New York, N.Y. 10017

ISBN: 0-373-05322-3

First Silhouette Books printing December 1986

America's Publisher of Contemporary Romance

Printed in the U.S.A.

LASS SMALL

started writing after attending a workshop where she received the following advice: "If you want to start writing, start." She did, and she's never looked back. In fact, she says, "I *love* writing. I love all aspects of it." When she's not writing the novels that have made her popular, she likes to spend her time reading, swimming and enjoying life with her husband and four children.

To Paul Lutus,
who programed the Apple Writer II quite brilliantly,
with my thanks.

And
to all the user groups with their proud hackers
who share their knowledge, card expansions
and innovations so generously.

And especially to
Fort Wayne Apple Computer Users Group,
an impressed salute.

One

It all began with a package of gum. None of it would have happened if Laura Fullerton hadn't decided she needed a specific kind if she was going to fly. She'd found her ears tended to block. However, Laura was at O'Hare Airport, there in Chicago, before she remembered the gum. That's when she ran into Tabitha, who'd been a sorority sister when they were at Indiana University in Bloomington. It was the first step.

"Laura!" Tabby called as if they were friends.

Laura turned about, vaguely recalling the voice, knowing whoever it was had to be an acquaintance. Calling her by name was an unarguable clue.

The aptly named Tabby was deliberately thin, and she was wearing a designer travel jump suit that looked smashing with her black hair and green eyes. It was a discreet golden color. She looked like a cover of *Vogue* in the days when women were being posed to resemble animals.

In contrast, Laura had on a smart navy business suit with a crisp shirt blouse, and her blond hair was in an efficient knot at the back of her head. Her walking shoes revealed she was not so new to air travel that she wasn't aware of the walking done in terminals.

"Where're you heading?" Tabby's teeth were normal; one always expected them to be small and feline.

"Columbia, South Carolina, via Atlanta."

"Oh, good. Give me your ticket and I'll switch your reservations—you'll still make your connection—and we can travel as far as Atlanta together."

Laura dredged up a smile.

So on that April day, the two women—who had only Greek letters in common—were sitting side by side in Chicago's O'Hare, that hub of world travel, waiting for their plane.

"How amazing to run into you." Tabby's green eyes studied her companion with the nonlethal interest of a well-fed cat. Tabby knew Laura had to be thirty, only a year young...uh older than Tabby. Tabby was avoiding thirty and had adjusted her age three times now. She noted Laura was still as slender as she'd been at eighteen and her hair looked suspiciously the same blond. Was it actually sun streaked? Or done cleverly so? And Laura's eyes hadn't ever been that blue. Were they really that color? Contacts were quite incredible these days, and a lot of people wore them to change or deepen the color of their eyes.

They talked rather inanely, for they were strangers, and Laura had been looking around at all the people striding purposefully, shuffling in lines, hurrying or waiting. "Ah, Tab, this life is remarkable. I've seen people I haven't seen in years. It seems to me everyone flies. Doesn't anyone just go to an office, work all day and go home at night? Does the whole world spend their lives flying from place to place?"

"You'll get used to it. The food isn't as good as it once was."

"How long have you been living this way, Tabitha?"

"For about—uh—since college. I was graduated young. Skipped a couple of grades . . . early on."

"You were always precocious," Laura commented dryly.

"Laura, do you wear contacts?"

"No. Why?"

"Don't you wear glasses at all?"

"No. Not yet. I come from a family of eagle-eyed people."

"Amazing." Tabby wasn't convinced.

"Do you know who I ran into last week? You'll never guess. She was a Tri Delt. Never mind guessing, I'll tell you. Ann Thompson!"

"Ann Thompson?" Tabby tasted the name. "Who's Ann Thompson?"

"Don't you remember? She married George Miller."

"I never knew any Ann Thompson. What'd she look like?"

"She's—"

The speaker came on: "Passengers for Miami flight—"

"That's us," Tabby said, rising.

"Atlanta, Jacksonville and Miami," the interrupted voice droned on.

They gathered their things and moved toward the line.

"Ann Thompson..." Tabby still chewed on that name trying to place her. It wasn't unusual for Tabby to have trouble recalling a woman.

"Ann Thompson...Miller," Laura added.

Then the second step in Laura's destiny occurred. Out of the crowd a man's voice intruded as he questioned, "Laura?"

"Pete? Why, hello!" Laura laughed as he leaned to kiss her. That flustered her, for she wasn't yet one of the kissing "hello" greeters.

He said cheerfully, "I only recently heard you and Tom split years ago. I'm just surprised it lasted as long as it did."

What was Laura supposed to reply to that? She hurried into chatter. "Tab, you remember Peter Watkins?"

Tabby remembered men and enthused, "Oh, yes! Hel*lo*!"

Her smile turned Cheshire briefly, to fade as Laura asked, "How's Molly?"

"Molly plus two babies." Peter dug for pictures.

It was comparatively easy to arrange their seats on board so that Peter was between them, and the talk was quick and animated until Peter asked, "Have you heard about Tanner? Or do you remember him?"

"Tanner? I remember him!" Tabby said in a perfectly normal way as though nothing had changed.

But Laura's face went still and cautious as if she realized it was the third step. "What about Tanner?"

"He was in a hell of a wreck. Completely totaled his Porsche. There wasn't any part that wasn't destroyed or at least bent." Pete shook his head.

"What about...Tanner?" Laura's breath was caught in her chest and her face was frozen. Her jaw didn't work right and her eyes weren't focused. The sounds around her were dimmed by a roaring in her ears and she saw Tanner quite clearly. He'd been tall, long-limbed, with dark tumbled hair and blue, blue eyes.

As from a distance, Laura heard Pete's reply, "Tanner? Oh, he's okay. He's down north of Myrtle Beach, at his parents' summer place. Been there awhile and probably will be for some time. He was given a leave of absence to recover. I doubt he'll ever get over losing..."

Laura gasped.

"...that Porsche. It was the perfect car. Was. That's the crucial word. What a mess. I saw pictures. Isn't it just like Tanner to have pictures of its demise? I've never seen a man so wrapped up in anything. Actually—" Pete slowly shook his head and his laugh was ironic "—it took them almost an hour getting him out of it. He was *really* 'wrapped up' in it. He'll probably have it burned, and spread the ashes on his place out in the wilds of lower Manhattan Island."

"New York?" Tabby frowned carefully.

"If you've ever been there, you know there's nothing wilder than New York." Peter was logical. "Tanner's family own some land there. It's under buildings, of course." He laughed, carried away by his imagination. "Some of the concrete jungle."

Laura's voice sounded faintly, "Is he . . . all right?"

"I haven't seen him. Charlie showed me the pictures of the car. Do you remember Charlie? I run into him a couple of times a year, here and there. He's a church *deacon*! Can you believe that? Charlie! Sells insurance. Last time I saw Charlie was in Denver. Do you suppose our whole class is flying around somewhere?"

"Yes." Laura could believe that. She was still in shock and impatient to find a way to bring Peter back to talking about Tanner.

"What are you doing now, Laura? Flying for pleasure or profit. What was your major?"

"She does paintings for lobbies." Tabby smiled at Peter for no more reason than the fact she always smiled at men.

"Oh." Pete had no idea what lobby paintings meant, and he wasn't terribly interested.

Laura elaborated, "I was an art major and I've done lobby paintings, but recently I've expanded. There's a group planning a chain of leisure houses. The chairman had seen some of my work and he's allowing me to try for the decoration contract. It's my first expansion project."

Pete nodded without a whole lot of interest and inquired, "Are you ladies going on to Miami?"

"I am." Tabby licked her lips to freshen her smile.

"No." Laura still wasn't focused. "My presentation is in Columbia, South Carolina."

"Hey! If you have time, you ought to drop over to the coast and see old Tanner. He's all alone down there."

"Tanner has never been alone in all his life." Laura's voice was just a little stiff.

Pete grinned. "He is now. He was getting burned out as it was. He was older than the rest of us, if you recall. His stretch in Nam put him in with us kids. Go over and say hello. He'll be grateful. The Moran place is easy to find. Just go north of Myrtle Beach out past Ocean Boulevard. It's a big old gray clapboard house. You can't miss it. Give him my regards and take a bouquet—here's the money." Pete slid his wallet out of his inside jacket pocket and removed a bill. "Give him this bouquet for his *Porsche*! He'll love it. I'll call him and tell him I'm sending a proxy to visit. Okay? Here's his address. You can just show up.''

Laura took the bill, but she was almost reluctant to commit herself to going. Should she? Should she go down and see Tanner again? The chatter continued between Pete and Tabby, and Laura must have contributed her share, but she was thinking of Tanner. She could go and see him. But should she?

Still occupied with the thought, Laura said goodbye to Pete and Tabby in Atlanta. She was aware that she was leaving Pete alone with Tabby, and the danger to Pete that entailed. But he was thirty, and he loved his wife and babies. He'd been flying around alone for years. He could take care of himself.

After that brief splinter of concern, her mind went back to The Question: Should she? How would it be to see Tanner again? How badly had he been hurt? And all through her presentation before the attentive board of directors, a corner of her mind was questioning: Should she?

She was still debating when she rented the car. By the time she was driving east on Highway 20 it occurred to her the debate was somewhat redundant. She was going.

Tanner. Just the name was enough to give the inside of her stomach deeply erotic shimmerings. She remembered when she first saw him around campus at I.U. in Bloomington, Indiana, and assumed he was a professor. He stood out even in the thirty-thousand-student maelstrom. He was older, smoother, he made all the other guys she knew look like high school visitors. Tanner.

He'd passed her one day as she crossed the shallow, narrow stream that divided the campus and was called the Jordan River, and he'd winked at her. She was immobilized. She turned like some kind of zombie programmed to simply trail along after him but he walked on with his long stride. She spent all day coaxing her nervous system to recovery.

That was the only time she'd ever seen him alone. He was always with other people. Laughing. He drew people like a magnet. Careless, easy, his smile so lazy and knowing. His dark hair mussed, his blue eyes amused by the world and everything in it.

Tanner would always wink at Laura when he saw her. Even surrounded by all those fawning women, he would wink at her. And it was like a kiss. It was a private thing just between them. She'd yearned over the idea of him. At night lying on her sagging mattress in the sorority house, listening to her roommate breathe in untroubled sleep, Laura would think about Tanner.

She'd met him so casually. There had been no heralding horns, no drum roll. She'd been standing with—who was it?—and Tanner had come up behind her. Then she had heard his actual voice and he'd said, "Well, hello. And who is this?"

She only remembered seeing his blue eyes with their incredible lashes looking down at her. Had she ever acknowledged the introduction? Probably not. She'd been stunned. Tanner shouldn't happen to a young, innocent woman. She had been too stupid to know what to do about him. She'd fumbled it. Botched her chance. But that's silly, she thought. She'd never had any real chance with Tanner.

He'd kissed her. That was what wrecked her whole facade of sophistication. Tanner's kiss had ruined her forever for any other man. So why was she driving through South Carolina in order to see him? Because she needed to confront this strange spell that had lingered for all these years. She would find out it had been a fantasy, and then she would be free of him. She needed to do this for her own sake. A dream can be a pleasant interlude for idle moments, or it can be crippling, making all other men seem lesser.

From the time she'd met him, she'd been helpless. An idiot. After that brief first meeting, he'd touched her shoulder as he left. He probably knew what chaos was racketing around in her body, and he escaped while he could still get away from her. He realized that if she'd ever managed to get her fingers unclutched from her stack of books, she'd have clutched them into him.

After that she noticed women always presumed too much around Tanner. They always had their hands on him. He didn't appear to mind. He was kind. He allowed it. They obviously needed it somehow. She thought they were all disgusting. Poor Tanner. But then she saw that he winked at others the same way he winked at her. It was like a casual smile to him. The wink was meaningless.

When he asked her out that first time, she'd just said yes to Mike. She went back to the sorority house and cried. But she knew that if she had gone with Tanner, she would have given him her soul. It was better to be safe with Mike than to get on the merry-go-round of madness that sharing time with Tanner would have done to her. Then Tanner graduated and was gone forever.

After she broke up with Mike, Tom asked her out, and she was already engaged to Tom when Tanner came back on campus to visit. He said he'd just heard she'd broken up with Mike and would she go with him? So she lost her only other chance to be with Tanner.

She'd had some bitter days. But Tom was sweet and she married him. Tanner had come to South Bend for the wedding. Quiet. Serious. He'd kissed her in the receiving line, and that was probably what ruined the honeymoon. Tom, well, that was all past.

She wondered if Tanner had ever married. He had to be thirty-five. How had he survived all these years? How had he survived Nam so unblemished? And now he'd survived a terrible wreck. What would it be like to see him again?

Would seeing him cure her? Or would it wreck her completely? She was light-years older now. Surely she would be able to speak and move when she was with him this time? She was a mature woman, capable of business presentations, good in her field, competent to cope with any situation. She had become used to directing other people and helping them to understand how things should look. She could communicate calmly under almost any circumstances and keep her head. What would seeing Tanner do to her?

What if he didn't know her from Adam...Eve. Pete hadn't told Tanner *who* was coming to see him. Only a proxy. Would Tanner stand there and look beyond her for the surprise? What was she doing driving now down Highway 501 in South Carolina all these years later, chasing a dream? A memory. A "might have been"?

Laura stopped at a florist in Myrtle Beach and bought a bouquet of red carnations with some fern. An anonymous arrangement, good for any occasion, she had decided. After that there was no reason to put it off, and she drove north on Ocean Boulevard and on out of town to the Moran "cottage."

She arrived toward evening. The house appeared to be on the highest knoll around where, unperturbed, it looked out on the great Atlantic Ocean. The palms rustled in their restless way as they strained the wind. The sky was overcast and the water curled in white horses that thundered onto the shore. The ocean. She had never been on a coast before.

In getting out of the car, she found she was a little stiff from sitting so immobile and tense while driving to Tanner. She stood straight, allowing her muscles time to adjust as she looked around. The house was gray clapboard with deep porches and wide windows that were open to the winds. There were spring's tulips carefully nurtured in beds around and about. And of course there was sand.

She took up the green, tissue-wrapped bouquet from Pete and went up onto the porch, deliberately making noise with her heels on the wooden steps and across the porch.

Had he heard the car? Would he be curious? Was he watching? She looked around at the view from the porch as if seeing him wasn't urgent, and as if her insides weren't trembling with her anticipation. She tried to appear as if this was a lark for her to come down here and see Tanner Moran.

She heard the door open and turned with a slight smile. So he *had* been watching. She saw he was dressed in soft, casual cottons, as he opened the screen, and he walked with one crutch. He came out, watching her, but he wasn't smiling. She was sure he didn't remember her.

"Hello, Tanner." He was even more devastating! Good Lord, what was she doing there?

"Laura." He said the name only.

"You do remember me." She managed her hostess smile, mutilating the flowers' stems between her two hands.

"Vividly."

"You look just the same."

"A bit battered. You look ... I can't believe you're here." His voice was soft. His face was still serious. There were laugh lines that were pale in his tan, to emphasize the fact that he wasn't smiling. Why was he so serious?

"I saw Pete on the plane from Chicago. He said you were here, so I drove over from Columbia. How are you?"

"Fine."

How inane. "Pete sent these to your *Porsche*." She laughed awkwardly and held out the flowers.

He took them, still watching her and said, "Thank you."

They just stood there. She wasn't sure what she should do. He hadn't invited her inside. He probably had a harem ensconced in there and didn't want this interruption.

"Come inside." It was as if he was only then conscious that he was host.

"Well ..." She shouldn't be too quick to go inside. She was bent on being casual.

"You drove down from Columbia? What were you doing there?" He held the door for her and she went on in.

The rooms distracted her from his questions. From the big center hall she could judge the house was larger than she'd first thought. Through doors she could peek into unused rooms where the furniture was draped with cotton dust covers for protection against the salt air, dust and sand. "This is perfect." She looked around. "Marvelous."

"It's like old silver and the patina of scratches that enhances it." He looked only at her. "The long years of living here have given the house a coating of love."

His word choice surprised her, she looked at him and her eyes then clung to him.

His marvelous deep voice went on like velvet, "We're the fourth generation to live in this house. My great grandparents bought it so all the grandchildren and their children could get together in the summers. This house is saturated with all the laughter and quarrels and gossip of a whole lot of relatives. Think what it could tell if it could talk." He grinned then. "You can see I've been alone for a while."

"I like the idea of all those lives linked here."

His eyes were steady on her. "Me too." Then he moved as if he'd caught himself staring and he asked, "And how is Tom?"

"He was fine, the last I heard."

"When was that?" He'd gone still again.

"Oh, three...no, four or so years ago. We were divorced after a couple of years."

"I hadn't known. I'd heard you were in business but no one ever mentioned a divorce. Have you remarried?" He watched her.

"No. Are you married?"

"No."

They both moved as if to break the tension. It must be her tension. Why would he be tense? He took Pete's flowers into the kitchen, and she trailed along as she'd longed to do all those years ago. He put the bouquet into an empty peanut butter jar and added water.

"I can't make the stairs but I can give you a tour of the lower floor. It's nicely laid out. Come and see." So he showed her around the rooms. The windows and doors were left open so that air moved and the place wouldn't be stale and musty. He walked, limping, supported by the crutch.

Being an artist, she naturally looked at the pictures on the walls. He told where they'd come from or who had painted them. They were almost all of the sea, palms, the house, sailboats or any combination thereof and were done by family members. All were charming and of a very wide range of talents.

Other than the pictures, the house primarily was colors to her. Fabrics were a new interest so those were noticed. She appreciated the rug lying like a jewel on the floor of the library, but flinched over the sand that it must endure in a beach house. The view out over the porch was magnificent and a sailboat rode the waves as if on cue.

For something to fill the silence, which she found awkward, but mainly to hear his voice again, she asked, "Where do you live ordinarily?"

"Wherever I'm working."

"Oh." She tried another tack. "Do you sail?"

"Not lately. Are you a sailor?"

"No." When they talked she had the excuse to look at him.

"You get seasick?" He smiled just a little.

"I've never tried sailing. I'm a landlubber. A prairie woman."

"We'll have to give you a taste while you're here. You can stay awhile? You're not due anywhere soon?"

"Well . . ."

"You would rescue me from terminal boredom." He was serious again.

"I can't believe you would ever be bored."

"I just discovered that I have been."

What did he mean by that?

"I can hold the door for you and carry your things across the porch, but stairs still throw me. I'm sorry."

"I have muscles." She grinned at him. He wanted her to stay with him?

"Muscles, huh? Don't intimidate me."

She laughed, putting her head back and enjoying the release from tension. Why had she been tense? He did want her to stay with him.

"You'd probably like a shower and more comfortable clothes? You did bring some knockabout clothes? If you didn't, we have a guest closet of almost anything, nothing designer but all well-worn, soft, broken in. You can dig through those."

How easily he assumed she would stay with him. Why not? It was a hospitable house, geared to provide for any oversight. There was certainly room enough, with casual, extra clothing in a guest closet . . . and the host was Tanner.

She wasn't sure she wanted to be that scruffy with him. She wanted to look pretty for him. But she would investigate the closet. There might be something wickedly intriguing. Something soft and sensual. In a guest closet? Come on, Laura, don't be silly.

Two

Tanner was still assimilating the fact: Laura Fullerton was actually there with him! She was real. He watched her as if she could disappear if he took his eyes from her for more than a brief second. It was unbelievable that she could be there, in that house and with him. He felt he shouldn't question it too closely, she might vanish. "Never doubt, accept." That's what his dad had always said.

How could any female look the way she did? Like a fragile princess in a tower. A lady. This was a dream. He didn't know quite how he should go about being alone with Laura Fullerton. He'd never had the chance when they were at I.U. There always seemed to be men around her. Male Neanderthals with their knuckles dragging and saliva dripping from their pointed teeth.

He smiled as he felt his own teeth pointing and his arms lengthening so his own knuckles would drag if she stayed around. She hadn't yet rejected his invitation to stay with him for a while. Would she? My God. If... All he had to do was remember which leg he was limping on.

She wouldn't let him carry her suitcase across the porch. "If you'll just hold the door?" Then she hesitated in the center hall, not knowing where she would go. She put down her bag and turned toward Tanner.

"I have one of the cooks' rooms at the back." He smiled. "Or," he said dismissively, "you can have any of the north rooms, those facing the top of the stairs. And there are the maids' rooms in the attic. No one else is here, so you have a wide selection."

He didn't want to crowd her in any way or have her feel threatened. He wanted her to feel as if whatever she did, it was by her own choice. That she was in control.

As he suspected, Laura was oddly uneasy. She'd never been in any situation even similar to this one, and she wasn't exactly sure how she should act, so she rushed into words: "In all of my life, I've never been on a coast."

He made his voice casual and a little slow. "You never went to Florida on spring break?"

Unknowingly she gave him an insight to her thinking. "I was quite strictly raised." There was a slight, telling pause before she went on. "Spring break I helped spring clean at home. My parents said that provided enough of a change. Actually it was fun. We had a good time. I have three sisters and we're all very close in age. They're cheerful. They all pitch in and work hard."

"I met them at your wedding."

"Oh, yes. I'd forgotten."

"I'm an only child."

"How horrible for you."

He smiled a little. "There were all these cousins." He gestured to indicate the big old house so often filled with relatives.

"Yes. Well, I'll go on up." But still she hesitated.

"Sorry I can't help."

Again she chattered, "I can handle it. I've learned to travel with only the essentials. Suitcase gallantry is apparently a thing of the past. I'll never forget a strong young man, carrying his little overnight bag, allowing me to struggle along with two weekenders and a garment bag in the Dayton airport. I send thoughts his way every now and then."

"He probably doesn't connect his rotten luck with his rudeness to you, and probably to a lot of other people, if he could have been so unkind to you." Tanner's tone was regretful because he hadn't been there to help her.

"That was my first trip. Perhaps his acting as ungentlemanly as he did was a lesson. Since then I've never taken more than *I* can handle alone. But I still don't like him. I think it was his smile. I would have learned anyway, when I found I had too much to carry by myself and help is so chancy.''

She smiled at Tanner, and with nothing else to delay her commitment—to actually going up the stairs and selecting a room—she quite bravely lifted her suitcase and carried it up the steps.

With that action she had selected the course of her life. It seemed so to her at the time, that she was doing something from which there was no retreat. She was choosing to do this rash thing. She was going to stay with Tanner, and... She couldn't think beyond the fact that she would be there with him. That was enough for now.

He stood watching her hips as she climbed the stairs. Lovely. He'd boxed himself in. He'd expected her to take one of the cooks' rooms downstairs. He'd said he couldn't climb stairs, but that wasn't quite true.

He called to Laura, ''The guest closet is one of the middle ones by the front bath. See it?''

''This one? Towels. This one. I found it.''

He measured his walk and the crutch thump carefully, for the sound in case she listened, as he went to the kitchen. It was a good thing the freezer was kept stocked. He heard the pipes rattle as she showered. He leaned against the counter and, with the predictable body reaction, ''saw'' her naked in that upstairs bathroom, and his mind ''watched'' her hands wash her body.

She was here in this house, and they were alone. She was going to stay with him. There was the chance he would make love with her. He groaned and turned to lean on his hands, spread apart on the counter, and he shook his head before he straightened and took deep breaths.

It was Laura, long ago, who'd inadvertently helped him hone the math rotes of tables and formulas he'd been forced to use to distract his mind from her.

He'd chopped the salad with a meat cleaver, thawed two steaks in the microwave and had charcoal smoldering in the grill out on the kitchen deck, when he heard her light steps coming down the back stair to the kitchen.

She called, "Brace yourself!"

He turned with an almost breathless anticipation, his grin beginning.

She opened the door at the bottom of the stairs and jumped down to spread her arms, as she exclaimed, "Ta-daaa!" She was a little overanimated in her effort to be casual.

She wore a man's shirt belted at the waist with a tie. It looked very like that was *all* she wore. And his mind became very busy when she lifted the shirt tails to expose purple running shorts that fit. So he didn't have a cardiac arrest after all. His grin broadened, mostly over his own reaction to her, but she thought he was being very nice and friendly.

"What can I do?" She immediately took in his preparations. "The table?"

"We don't eat out of the skillet?" He pretended surprise.

"Tacky," she pronounced haughtily as she dug into drawers and opened cabinets to find what was needed. "I should have known you were running around loose long ago. I might have recovered faster."

Rather sassily she inquired, "Been coping with ptomaine from eating from unwashed skillets?"

"I am meticulous. I *always* wash my eating utensils. I like your hair up that way."

"I couldn't find any more pins."

"I'll go up later and see if I can't find some somewhere."

"I thought you couldn't climb stairs." She paused to look at him.

"While carrying suitcases," he reminded her quite cleverly and smiled only a little as if being polite.

"I see." She gave him a careful look.

They ate on the deck on a round metal table where they'd put Pete's flowers. The table was rather battered but handy, and it fit perfectly in one corner of the deck where the rail benches met. Trees grew close to the deck and their branches were a leafy shade for those using it, but they could still see through the trunks of the trees to the ocean. It was a lovely setting.

He scorched the steaks and she took hers back and cooked it. He couldn't understand what was revolting about all the succulent juices that collected on his plate or why she averted her eyes. He thought that was funny.

She enjoyed the chopped salad and savored the Tanner Moran dressing. When she questioned him about the ingredients, he tried to remember what he'd put into it. The variety of spices and herbs he mentioned was outrageous. She was not quite sure if she should believe him. He was astonished she'd doubt him.

In describing the dressing, Tanner would take up a tiny bit of the lettuce, then he'd squint his eyes and move his tongue around his lips as he considered what was in the dressing.

She watched his tongue. She wasn't thinking about ingredients for a salad dressing; she thought about his tongue on her. How shocking.

After they had eaten, she found half a fresh apple pie in the refrigerator. "Do you bake?"

"No, there's a nice little lady, a neighbor, who looks in on me now and then." His face was bland.

"We have neighbors like that in South Bend." She busily cut wedges and added some vanilla ice cream. Leaning on his crutch, he held the door as she carried their desserts out to the metal table. With the first bite she was impressed. "Your neighbor is a jewel." She closed her eyes and made a very throaty sound of relishing the pie.

"She's very helpful." He smiled as the fine hair on his back rose along his spine while he listened to her sound of enjoyment. My God, would she react to him that way?

"I think I need to know her secrets."

"I . . . would doubt she'd share them with you." He was more amused than the words warranted.

She chose to take his statement at face value. "I know cooks like that. They'll give you the recipe all right and just neglect to give a vital ingredient so yours turns out rotten. I'm not a natural cook."

"You cooked the bloody hell out of that steak."

She nodded judiciously. "Aptly chosen words."

"I'm quick," he agreed.

"Are you? I only remember all the people who crowded around you in school. And how disillusioning it was when I found out you winked at everyone. You haven't winked at me since I got here."

"I'm saving it for effect."

"Really?" She gave him a careful look. "A whammy?"

"A try."

"I'll have to brace myself." She turned her attention back to the pie.

"I intend to catch you unaware."

"Warned?"

"Anticipation?"

"Now, Tanner . . ." She stopped and looked at him again.

"Did I ever tell you that no one has ever said my name the way you do?"

"Tanner?"

"The first time you said it about knocked me sideways."

"You patted my shoulder."

"I kissed you," he corrected. "But you didn't kiss me back."

"I'd never met anyone like you." Her tone was very serious. "You just kissed me without any warning. I wasn't prepared."

"You have to be warned?" He moved a bit closer and watched her pupils expand. She didn't move away. He leaned over and gently kissed her lips. "Hello, Laura." His voice was low and reedy with desire.

She swallowed and opened her eyes but he kissed her again, wrecking his entire nervous system, pointing his teeth and allowing his lengthening arms to wind around her twice.

"Tanner..." But she slowly shook her head and her eyes were very serious. "Don't make a move on me yet."

There was the "yet." He took a deep breath and said, "Hold very still and don't say anything exciting."

"Exciting? Like what?"

"Oh, you know: hello, or how are you, or it's going to rain...anything like that."

She grinned and made a scoffing sound.

"Your lips move when you speak and I think of them moving under mine." He was completely serious. If he'd been only flirtatious, it wouldn't have been so unsettling to her.

Self-conscious, she quickly licked her lips then looked at him and parted them to protest she hadn't meant anything by doing that, but he kissed her again.

"Now, Tanner..."

And of course he replied, "Great!" and shoved the table back to rise. He had to remember to reach for the crutch.

"No!" she protested.

"I'll probably go stark, staring mad with you around here." He grinned. "And I can't even jog."

"Awwww."

"I find sympathy erotic."

She gave him a companionable swat to the shoulder and said, "Stiff upper lip and all that sort of rot, old man."

But she sent him into a rumble of laughter that he fought to control.

"You silly," she said with a commendable show of casual tolerance as she got up.

Handling the crutch quite easily, he helped carry their dishes into the kitchen to add to the dishwasher. "Thank God you arrived."

She glanced at him in quick inquiry.

"Alone, I could never fill the dishwasher." He grinned. "You thought I was going to say something else, didn't you."

"Well, the state of the dishwasher hadn't really occurred to me as being a problem to discuss."

"I never dreamed you would divorce. I thought when you married it would be for life."

"Me, too." She started the dishwasher. "What about you? I can't understand why you've never married."

"I've been too busy. Too involved in...rather complicated...operations in...apprehending...uh... tricky people. White-collar crimes."

Replying was obviously a courtesy to her, but he really didn't want to talk about it. He was giving minimal information and wouldn't volunteer much on his own. There was a thoughtful silence before she asked cautiously, "What do you do for a living?"

"I investigate strange occurrences."

"Like...?"

"Oh, like money where there shouldn't be any. Strange traffic patterns. People in odd places. That sort of thing."

"Dangerous work?"

"Rarely."

She had expected him to say no. "What do you mean...rarely?"

"For the most part citizens are law abiding, then there are those who choose to be clever. When they're caught it's like Monopoly—they go to jail or forfeit a bundle. No big deal. They tried it but got caught. White-collar crimes. On occasion, someone will have real criminal reactions: they weren't guilty, they were *caught*, and they get mad at the catcher. That can be very, very nasty."

"This wreck you were in . . ."

"It's being investigated quite carefully."

"By whom?"

"My organization."

She guessed. "You'd rather I not pry?"

"There's nothing to tell."

"I . . . see." She leaned against the counter and they were silent for a minute or two. Soberly she said, "I'm surprised that I'm here. I shock me a little."

"I remember the first time I saw you at I.U. crossing our River Jordan, and you were wearing a blue shirtwaist when all the other girls were in shorts or jeans. And my dreams were filled with you. The one class I had with you—ethics, for God's sake—I never heard one word of that class. I sat two rows back and one seat over from you so I could feast my eyes on you. My eyes consumed you and you didn't even know it."

"Tanner," she cautioned.

"Just take it easy. You will let me kiss you goodnight?"

"I'm not sure that would be wise."

His eyes crinkled. "I can control myself. I'm a mature adult. You needn't be afraid of me."

"No blundering into the wrong bedroom looking for the bathroom in the middle of the night?"

"Promise." He held up his right hand in solemn pledge.

"Well, when it's bedtime, I'll let you kiss me good-night." With her agreement, there was a shimmer of anticipation at the thought of his kiss.

He suggested, "We could practice."

She was briefly startled, then she gave him an amused, chiding look.

He argued, "If I only get one good-night kiss, what if I louse it up? That could ruin my whole evening! We ought to practice." He was completely logical.

"Tanner—" she shook her head and sighed a bit broadly "—you're really pushing it."

"Oh yes."

"Cut it out."

He slumped very dispiritedly.

"Have you tried the stage?"

"Oh, was the dejection well-done? I've really never needed to practice." He gave her a sly and foxy look that made her laugh.

He remembered the crutch as they went into the living room. There was a folding card table, beautifully made of cherry wood. On it lay a partially done jigsaw puzzle. Laura was drawn to it. And they spent almost an hour slowly fitting pieces, until she yawned too many times.

Reluctantly she said, "It's been a long day and I must go to sleep."

"Good. Now I get my kiss."

She grinned at him. "You really shouldn't just leap into such an experience, you should approach it gradually. Kiss my hand the first night, then my cheek..."

"Let's read ahead a week or two."

"My mother always said nothing worthwhile is ever accomplished in a hurry. Everything takes time."

"Yes."

"Would you like to kiss me now?"

"Will it count against the good-night kiss?"

"It would *be* the good-night kiss."

He watched her with narrowed, suspicious eyes that held humor. "By any chance are you working as a part of a revenge group that I've helped corner somewhere along the way?"

She agreed airily and invented a mob. "Maxie and Bugsy and uh..."

"I knew it." He played along with her imagination. "They must have hunted you down knowing it was fated that I had a good-night kiss long overdue. What did they bribe you with to come here to torture me this way?"

"Rubies, emeralds and pearls?"

"Don't you believe them. They had to give it all back. With fines. They won't be solvent enough for this kind of caper for years yet."

Having said all that about honor, it amused him to drag the crutch over to use as help in rising. He did it well. Then he reached out a hand and tugged Laura to her feet. "I have to lean against the wall," he told her. "Because I want to hold you with both arms."

She bought it. He propped the crutch nearby, not overdoing it, and then took her into his arms. Quite easily he had reminded her he'd been badly injured and her sympathy had been touched. He pulled her closer, holding her, feeling her against him. Relishing her there. His strong hands moved on her back and up her sides in a very insidious way.

He hugged her, prolonging it exquisitely, making her wait. Making her aware of him. Making her aware of herself and her reaction to him. He was merciless. He had no idea how long he could keep her there in that house with him, and he had to use any opportunity that came his way.

He figured if he wasn't going to sleep that night, then neither was she. Deliberately he brushed his lips over hers. She lifted hers to return his kiss, but he drew back an inch to say, "I had to be sure they were there. Since I get only one, I'd hate to blunder and miss entirely."

She didn't break position and left her mouth where it was. She hadn't really listened to his words. She was being distracted by the shimmer of tiny, pulsing thrills.

He ran his evening's beard down her cheek and under her ear. His hot breath rasped in his throat and she felt it almost roar in her ear as he said urgently, "I lost your mouth. Is it around here?"

Somehow she managed to form the words: "Over here." Her own breathing was unsteady. He had her completely concentrated on him. The sensations that flickered through her body were electric in her reaction to him. How clever he was. She wanted more of him.

He whiskered the side of her throat in his search for her mouth, and his hands moved on her back. He braced his legs apart and pulled her closer, his hands went down her back and he drew her tightly to him.

It was then he finally got around to kissing her. The kiss concentrated Laura's attention to the need he'd built in her. She was a shambles. Her lips clung to his as he tried to ease from the kiss and it continued long past what had been her deadline. He was wickedly pleased.

But worse, he insisted on breaking off the kiss. He even helped her to stand away from him. He loosened her resisting arms from around his shoulders and held her reaching hands politely between them. Then he lifted them and kissed them. He explained, "The first night and hand kissing. Do I get to still kiss hands tomorrow? Or only cheeks by then?" And he grinned at her.

She replied something unintelligible as she swallowed with some difficulty.

He patted her bottom as he started her up the stairs. She hesitated and looked back, but he only said, "Good night, Laura."

She said, "Ummm."

He was jubilant. His conscience didn't even twinge.

Three

It wasn't until after she was in bed, lying there in the dark room, that Laura really became aware of her surroundings. She'd scrubbed her teeth, braided her hair into two pigtails and changed into her night wear of T-shirt and panties before she began to realize how big the house was . . . and how isolated.

At that point her awareness lay in hearing sounds that were different for her. First to capture her attention were the unusual ones of the surf and the palms rustling and rattling in the almost constant breezes. Other sounds reminded her that the house was old and wooden, and the creaking was like a ship groaning through a gentle sea.

She was too tired to allow her imagination to interpret any of the other sounds. She shunned the possibility that the old house could well be haunted. She did permit herself some questioning as to why she was where she was. The Fullertons' daughter, Laura, doing this rash and reckless thing?

To be here alone with a man she hadn't seen in seven years, well, actually six years, nine months and twelve days. How interesting—how telling—that she couldn't remember how long it had been since she'd last seen her ex-husband, but she could remember exactly how long since she'd last seen Tanner. It was the day she married Tom Bligh, and Tanner Moran had ruined her honeymoon with his reception line kiss.

How could a human man kiss so perfectly? Her body wasn't curious about analysis, it just craved more. She moved restlessly under the onslaught of reaction that flickered like summer lightning in her passion-drugged cells. There had to be something genetic about his talent. What if scientists could splice a gene to duplicate Tanner's talent for kissing? Nobody would get anything else done.

Life, however, consisted of more than just reaction to kisses. She really didn't know Tanner well enough to have committed herself to visiting him alone in this enormous summer house. He could have changed.

His kisses hadn't. But what about his character? She had changed since she knew him; perhaps he had, too. The years between twenty-five and thirty-five were the

years that molded character. How old was he exactly?
She went to sleep trying to figure that out.

Her body's senses had lain there smoldering like
coals lightly covered with the ash of hidden fire. The
wind of her dreams stirred the ash covering and allowed the oxygen of her imagination to feed the dormant embers and blow it again to flame.

She made restless sounds and movements as the
longing intensified but the dream-Tanner was elusive.
How unkind of him to tease and torment her.

There was a loud bang. It couldn't be a car's back-
fire, not on that deserted road. A shot? It must have
been a door slamming. Whatever it was, it brought her
almost to the surface of her dream state, and in the
brief rousing, she thought she heard a woman's laugh.
But she ignored that puzzle as she tried to sink back
into her alluring fantasy. In searching again for her
dream, she slid into deeper, restful sleep.

Tanner waited for her to sleep. Her bed had
squeaked with her entry, and his longing for her
flamed vividly. He almost put the crutch aside and
only just avoided pacing—and disturbing that creaky
floor. He again took up the crutch and moved with its
sound to his room. He put it by the bed before he released the window screen, slid over the sill, to the
ground, melted into the night, and walked carefully
with his healing muscles.

He didn't yet run. He'd been promised that the time
would come when he would run again. How ironic to

have been a year in Nam, without a scratch, to almost
be wiped out in a car wreck. How miraculous to have
survived that incredible wreck without brain damage.
Not only did he survive but, as bad as the damage to
him was, he would heal. He had a little metal in some
bones now, and there would be some interesting scars,
but he would be all right.

Right now the scarring was pretty ugly. If—no,
when he made love to Laura, he should do it in the
dark. She could be turned off by the sight of his
wounds. They didn't bother him; he was just glad he
was alive. There had been some question of survival.
He'd come to, lucid, fantastically aware. Sounds were
so clear. The colors sharp. There was no distortion.
He'd known he was alive!

Then he looked at himself. If he was still alive, and
it was no illusion, he could be saying farewell to his
life. His body was in very bad shape. His left arm at
strange angles. His stomach was a mess. The thigh ...
He touched his stomach, but he had to stop walking
to lean down and hold that thigh as if reassuring himself it was still there...and thank God it was. How had
he been so fortunate?

All his life he would send blessings to the people
who helped him. The fragile-appearing woman who
had wiggled into the car, as close as she could get to
Tanner, and snaked an arm over to hold the pressure
point. She had kept him from bleeding to death before they got him out. She had talked to him calmly,
explaining what had happened, what they were doing

and how. She told him who they'd called to come help, and she'd told him that he would live.

There was a brute of a man who was so gentle and who wept for him. The contrasts. Why wasn't the brute the one who was businesslike and the woman leaking tears? Why must we go through horrendous trials before we know how compassionate and unselfish people are?

All through the struggle to release him, there had been the threat of explosion. The fire truck couldn't get there to wash down the car for more than half an hour. His rescuers would have waited for the experts. They would have left him alone except for stopping the bleeding. But they had to try to free him before the car blew up.

No one was so unmindful as to just grab him and try to yank him out. Too many people are harmed by inept good intention. It was the threat of explosion that made them try to bend the metal, to pry space so they could get him away.

Tanner learned later that the man who'd crossed the centerline going mindlessly pell-mell was killed. They were generally the ones who survived. That time the victim survived. Tanner had used up another of his nine lives.

And now Laura was there in his house.

He didn't sleep well that night. He was more restless than he'd ever been. He lay awake thinking about his restlessness, and he wondered if it was because now he knew how tentative life was. He'd learned that it

was not to be wasted. He'd had that lesson under-
lined for him. And with Laura there, had he a chance
to fill his gift of life with love?

Could she love him?

He was awake early. He got up and dressed, wearing a long-sleeved, cotton shirt and soft cotton deck
trousers to hide the scars, and he remembered to carry
the crutch along. He checked his messages, for he
never took a straight phone call. He returned a few
and erased the rest. He worked on his computer, with
its involved system of codes, and he took coffee out on
the kitchen deck. A strange almost melancholy mood
had seized him. Could she love him? Why should she?

In that early-April dawn's stillness, with its soft taste
of summer, she came to him out of the kitchen door
with her hair brushed down around her shoulders. She
was wearing a wraparound dress of cotton. The lime
green with dark blue print made her eyes a strange
slate color. She wore someone's thongs from the guest
closet, and as the almost summerlike breeze molded
the soft dress against her body, she had to lift her hand
to brush away the strands of her silken hair from
across her face. She smiled at him, making his heart
hurt.

"Don't get up," she told him quickly.

"I didn't think you'd waken this early."

"I'm a morning woman. I love the early hours. Of
course, then I tend to fade out early in the evening."

"I could hear you snore clear down here."

"How unkind of you to mention that." She gave him a sparkling-eyed, humorous snub that was pure sass.

"What do you eat for breakfast?"

"Everything in sight."

"A woman after my own heart." Such careless, flirting words, but he lowered his eyes quickly so she wouldn't see how vulnerable she made him. "I make the world's best waffles."

"I do bacon and eggs."

"How?"

"Any way at all."

"We'll combine."

They went inside and as they emptied the dishwasher and put away last night's dishes, Laura asked, "Who cleans this place?"

"A cleaning crew. Top to bottom once a month. They vacuum and mop and change the dust covers. There are ten of them. It's safest for us bystanders to just leave—you could find yourself mopped up or with a cover thrown over you. But don't panic, they aren't due until the first of May."

The waffles were frozen and commercial, so he had time to lean against the counter and watch her do all the rest. When all was ready, they again ate on the deck, and she laughed. "Imagine all that house and we eat outside on this old wooden deck."

"You can begin painting it tomorrow."

"You're giving me a whole day of rest!" she exclaimed.

"That's because you're non-union."

"Speaking of work, I need to report in. And I've some drawings to do. I'll need a large space. Do you have a recreation room? A game table?"

"I have a drafting table I'm not using," he offered.

"Incredible."

"I can arrange for anything your heart desires." He leaned back and crossed his arms on his broad chest as he watched her intently. "I can construct, provide or commandeer whatever you need."

"Well, with that offer I believe I could use a sampling of silks in all the colors, some swatches of sample patterns, tempera paints. Brushes, of course. And a good electric pencil sharpener. Butcher paper. You know, the kind of things all artists need." And she laughed because her request was ridiculous. "Actually, if you have a drafting table, I have what I need for these next several days. Where's your phone?"

"I'll have to show you." He stacked the plates. "I have some small modifications on the system but it's only the matter of a couple of switches. This way the phone never rings."

"You're allergic to phones?"

"To time wasters."

She could see where, having been through that wreck, he wouldn't want intrusions on what must be precious time. They dealt with the dishes, then she followed along to the study. He showed her the main phone and how to flip the whole ensemble back into being a plain, ordinary phone.

"What *is* all this? I have a message taker, but this is silly. What are all these gadgets?"

"A filter, a scrambler, a tracer and a few other little odds and ends."

She frowned and gave him a careful look. "A... scrambler?"

"Some of the information I receive is confidential."

"Secrets?"

"Well, people's financial information, or private numbers. Nothing exciting. Just personal."

"Oh." She picked up something reasonably similar to a phone and asked, "Now?"

"Sure. Those are the switches. If you use the phone, flip them to off. See? Let me know if you do use the phone so I can be sure they're back on and working. Okay?"

"I just have to report in. I won't give this number."

"You can call out anytime." He didn't move but leaned against the wall with his crutch and quite blatantly listened.

She was amused by him, as she sought and punched the speaker button so he could hear both sides of the conversation. She wondered if he would allow her the same privilege? No, he couldn't. If he could, there wouldn't be the scrambler.

She punched in the number, and Jeanine—her secretary—immediately answered. "Laura? How'd it go?"

"Looks good. I got the go-ahead for mock-ups. It will be interesting. I'm staying with friends on the coast and will do some of the preliminary sketches here. I'll call every day about noon? There's no phone for any other calls. Everything okay?"

"Fine. How long will you be gone?"

"Good question. I'll let you know."

When she'd hung up and watched as Tanner adjusted all the switches, he asked, "I guess I didn't ask what you do?"

"I was an art-design major. I did portraits first because that's my love. But lately I've expanded into decoration, coordinating color and texture for specific places and moods. It's fascinating, different, a challenge, but I'm not sure it's exactly what I want to do.

"My first big job was to decorate a company's holiday house for guests and selected employees who'd pleased the boss. It's on the shore of Lake Michigan. It's big enough, but a small house compared to this one, and I was told to use my own judgment. So I fixed it up as the ideal place for a vacationing family. Sunflowers in the breakfast room, teddy bears and balloons in the smaller bedrooms, pretty flowered wallpaper in the master bedroom. It was all fresh and clean. I finished and reported to the owner.

"He came by my studio in South Bend, looking placid and bland. He waited until we were alone and then he said, 'I believe there's been some kind of misunderstanding. When I said the place was for week-end fun, I didn't mean for a *family* but for fun and *games*. Now do you understand? For men to take women who aren't their wives.'"

Tanner smiled. "You innocent. What did you do?"

"After an almost overwhelming episode of blushes and stuttering, I said, 'Oh,' and eventually managed to stammer that I'd take care of it."

"And...?"

"The teddy bears went first, then the balloons and sunflowers. I found the whole project distasteful but I felt committed to correct my error. I changed the colors, put in mirrors and as a rather wicked afterthought, lacy palms. An upright piano." She paused. "I resisted the black woven string and tasseled door hangings."

"Noble. Did he try to get you to initiate it with him?"

"How could you *possibly* have known that?"

"I know you didn't and that he's still after you, right?"

"Yes." She watched him a minute before she asked curiously, "How could you know? Is this typical male behavior? He has a wife and half-grown children. He's a corporate power. Why me? His wife is a very nice woman. She likes him. I think he likes her. Why does he want to fool around? And why with me? I'm hardly the type to be a mistress. At best I'd be inept. I've been very businesslike and formal with him, I've never flirted or teased him. I've never brushed up against him or indicated in *any* way that I would be interested.

"And since then, I make sure what sort of place I'm supposed to decorate. I've refused two other 'fun' places. I don't want any part of something like that. And although I accept jobs from him and his referrals, I don't feel obligated to sleep with him to 'repay' him. My work is excellent. I've won awards...."

Tanner's eyelashes screened his eyes as he said mildly, "He was probably surprised to find a woman who can still blush, and that intrigued him. Plus the fact that you *didn't* try to attract him."

She scoffed. "Ridiculous. You're saying that in order to be free of him I should try to entice him and..."

"No!"

"Well you just said..."

"You're handling the situation in the most professional way possible. You're doing it exactly right. Don't be too friendly, stay courteous and business-minded when you have to talk to him."

"You're a man, why would he want to fool around?"

"I'm prejudiced." He meant prejudiced about her attractiveness and how she affected him.

"So you think whatever men do is okay?"

He shook his head. "That isn't what I said."

"You said that you're prejudiced. Do you go after every woman within your scope? Do you trail after them and hunt them down?"

"I've always been selective."

"But—"

"I can only say I admire the man's taste in women."

She smiled just a bit. "Do you find me attractive?" The words were out before she could stop them, and she was appalled!

"Unbelievably so."

"Why, how nice of you!"

"I'm not sure about 'nice.'"

"I know, you want me to help 'initiate' this house? I would suspect there have been others who've made love here."

He licked his lips slowly then intoned, "It's worth being sure. Consider all the cousins here with their parents. It's very doubtful there's ever been the privacy for any love making, only furtive, hasty sex." He shook his head sadly. "That's probably why the house sighs and creaks so restlessly. It's unfulfilled."

She laughed. She had to put her head back to laugh. "Oh you!" she gasped and put her hands to her face and the laughter bubbled from her. "You're so clever! I probably would have succumbed to him if he'd been as clever as you! You're so inventive!"

"I can be exquisitely so." He allowed a small smile.

She sobered a little and looked at him. Her own smile was still there. A soft, inviting one. But her eyes were still a bit wary.

He took her into the morning room and showed her the drawing table with its high "Bob Cratchit" stool.

"It seems unusual for you to have a drafting table. Who used it?"

"We needed something high enough to keep puzzles, community scissors, papers and so on away from small children. By the time they could stretch up to the top of it, or climb up, they would know enough to leave things alone. Our family tends to have hobbies that involve small things or sharp things or dangerous things."

"How dangerous? Poison mushrooms?"

"Guns, knives, scissors."

"Guns?" she asked in surprise.

"We've lived on this coast for a long, long time and it's isolated. Then one uncle became intrigued by the progression of weapon utility. The innovations in weaponry. Some are exquisitely ornamental. We have an extensive gun collection that is now concealed and protected very securely. They'll eventually go to a museum."

"Guns scare me."

He told her, "It's like dealing with rattlesnakes. You do it carefully."

"I can shoot one."

"I won't tempt you to try."

"My dad said we should all know how. One never knows what sort of cards life deals you."

"Logical." He nodded with his words.

"So I *can* shoot one. But I don't ever want to. I'm dreadfully afraid of them."

"There'll be no need. I'll take care of you." He moved to her carefully, carrying the crutch, and he slid an arm around her unresisting body to pull her to him. Their eyes locked, and slowly he leaned his head down and kissed her.

Being close to him wasn't any different. She felt the same old chaos. The same maelstrom of sensation. Plain, ordinary rioting of cells. Body disaster. So how could she resist? She kissed him back.

For some reason, unknown to her, he released her. She carefully re-sorted her brain cells to figure out why he'd done such a foolish thing, when he suggested they return her car to the rental branch in Myrtle Beach. She had to blink several times in the reorientation process before she could ask, "Can you drive all right? I mean, will it hurt your leg?"

"No problem. Only my left leg gives me trouble. My right leg's fine."

"You don't mind following me in and bringing me back?"

"Not at all. I'd be happy to do it." He could hardly wait to get rid of her means of escape.

As they returned to the Moran cottage, he drove along a track close to the ocean, and she relished doing that. "I think I must have been a pirate in another life."

"A past life or a parallel one?" he inquired.

"Parallel? I hadn't considered that. I was thinking a past one."

His glance touched her hotly as she looked out over the rolling waves, with the wind streaming her hair back and molding the thin cotton to her chest. "Being a pirate could come in handy under many circumstances."

"What would you steal?" she asked. "Treasure?"

"You."

She laughed as if he was teasing.

He wasn't.

Four

———

Laura spent the day working in the "silence" of only natural sounds. She could hear no motors or buzzes or ringings. She didn't even hear any relentless wind chimes. The Moran place was truly isolated.

In Columbia, Laura had been given a stack of floor plans for the leisure houses. She had been one of several decorators offered the opportunity to show what could be done with color and texture to make identical layouts look individual.

She jotted down some general ideas: old-fashioned, Oriental, stark colored, contemporary. And with the great selection offered by the crayons, she began to experiment, making pencil notes on the borders, lost to her imagination.

Her stomach mentioned lunch was lacking. She surfaced from her work and lifted her nose to sniff. Chili? She laid her pencil aside, swung around on the stool and left the table to follow the aroma into the kitchen where Tanner was stirring a pot on the stove.

He looked up at her. "I thought chili would do it. I was pretty sure it needed to be something with a tantalizing smell. My goodness, you do concentrate! Did you notice I changed you and your table to another room?"

Her expression was blank for just a brief minute before she smiled. "No you didn't." But she was sure only because she could actually recall coming from the morning room. "Toast?"

"With melted cheese and in the warmer."

"I'm famished."

"It's the sea air. I suppose, after you've been here awhile, I'll have to widen all the doors so you can waddle through."

"Ummmm." She was sampling the toast.

"Don't take my corners," he warned.

"You're a toast corner devotee?"

"Yep. We had an old cat who recognized any sound that involved the toaster and would come a-waddling for the corners. I didn't discover toast corner madness until I was twelve! I'd been psyched out by that old cat into thinking the corners were only for him!"

As Laura began to scoff, there was a call from beyond the kitchen deck. "Tanner! Come help."

Laura followed Tanner's hobble to the door and looked past his shoulder to see a tiny blonde labor up the deck stairs, her arms burdened with packages and baskets.

"It's my neighbor," Tanner explained as he opened the door. "Hi, what'd you bring me this time?"

This time? So *this* was the neighbor who baked that pie? Um-hmm. And the neighbor who probably wouldn't "share her secrets" with Laura? No wonder Tanner had laughed when he told her that. What sort of secrets had she been showing Tanner?

The Other Woman—her title was already in capital letters—looked dismissively at Laura and said, "I do hope you're not here for lunch, there's only enough for two." And she smiled sweetly at Tanner.

Possession is nine points of the law and, being in residence, Laura stepped back and held the door with a courteously welcoming smile pasted on her face. "Well, hello!" she said to the intruder. "Are you the apple pie? Or the quiche?" She'd fabricated the quiche and was pleased she thought of it.

"Quiche?" The woman's lovely face was blank. "No quiche." And, ignoring Laura with polished talent, she went on into the kitchen with pointed familiarity.

Quite remarkably, Tanner didn't ask about a nonexistent quiche. But he smiled just a little. Laura gave him a precious look that made him cough discreetly, as if with a throat tickle, before he said, "Laura, this is my neighbor, Pam Howard. My house guest, Laura Fullerton.''

"House guest?" Pam then did pause to pierce Laura with a narrow-eyed look.

Her face commendably placid, Laura explained, "Old school friends."

Pam smiled. "I have just begun to notice how older women search out unmarried school acquaintances."

"Have you been successful?" Laura inquired kindly.

Apparently Tanner had another throat tickle.

Pam ignored Laura and said sweetly to Tanner, "I thought we'd go out on the beach. You do have a rug we can take along? Don't you have a clay wine cooler? I brought your favorite..."

"Moonshine? Where'd you find some?"

"...chablis." Pam looked a little miffed.

"I love chablis," Laura contributed in a friendly way. "If it's dry enough. But we have some red wine for the chili. Don't we, darling?"

That was very bold of Laura. And he *was* amused. However, although she wasn't looking at him, she was waiting for his reaction to the "darling."

He replied readily enough, "Let's ask her to join us, shall we, honey?"

Had there been just the least bit of hesitation to emphasize the "honey"? He was wicked. Of the choice in responses to asking Pam to join them, which should she select? Not "no." It would seem insecure. "If you want to" would appear as if Tanner would choose to have Pam there. So Laura smiled brilliantly as she exclaimed, "I insist!" Then she turned to Pam and begged, "Oh, do stay! It'll be such fun."

What could Pam do? They didn't go to the beach, but instead ate in the kitchen. Laura put out two glasses each for the kinds of wine and they had a smorgasbord. It should have been fun.

However, when Pam relentlessly spoke of things Laura knew nothing about, Tanner supplied *elaborate* backgrounds to each comment. He was enjoying himself, and his eyes shared that with Laura.

So when Pam tried to shut Laura out by speaking in French, Laura absentmindedly corrected her grammar as she pulled some meat from a drumstick and examined it with a critical frown.

Pam didn't stay long. She insisted Tanner help her carry her baskets home, but he was using the crutch and simply put out his hands helplessly. Laura volunteered her help, even insisted, but she was ignored. Pretending Pam was behaving, Laura waved her off from the deck. However Pam neglected to look back so didn't know to return the wave.

"My, my," Tanner said. "I would never have dreamed you could hold your own with Pam. And there I'd worried she would make mincemeat out of you."

"As a sophomore, in the sorority's schedule, I was assigned to room six weeks with Tabby. You must remember Tabby Cat? I had a six-week crash course in cattiness. She was a senior then and two years older than me. On my way down to Columbia, she spotted me in Chicago's O'Hare and I had a quickie refresher course. I also found out she's now three years younger than she was before.

"Pete was on the same flight out of O'Hare. He did call you?" she asked Tanner. "He said he was going to. Do you know that innocent is only thirty and only been out on his own for eight years in the wilds of air travel and I left him to the tender mercies of *Tabby*?" She put a hand to her forehead. "They were both going to Miami. I dread to think of him now, almost forty-eight hours later. Poor Pete."

Humor radiated from Tanner's eyes and, restraining his grin, he shook his head. "Poor Pete." But he didn't sound sincere.

Predictably Pam had left before the kitchen was tidied. As the two straightened it up, Tanner stretched over for something to add to the dishwasher. His shirt rode up and Laura saw the dreadful, healing scars on his left side. She laid her hand there and said, "You should strip down to shorts and get those outside in the sunlight and fresh air. I suppose the new skin is too tender for sunbathing?"

When she touched him, he'd frozen, braced for her horror. And his relief over her natural reaction was intense. "I could stand a little time on the lounge in the shade of the deck. Come on out with me."

"I won't chat. I'll go to sleep. I suppose it's the sea air. I slept like a dead woman last night."

"I'm glad I don't revolt you," he said softly.

"Oh, no. I was a candy striper volunteer in the surgical ward back at the age when everyone was going to be either a doctor or a veterinarian. Hospital people think of scars as successes, so I learned to look on them that way too instead of anguishing over the hurt that caused them."

He was very conscious of her as they moved out to the deck. He was a little stiff and nervous. He took off his shirt and spread it on the plastic padding of the double lounge, sat down and patted the other side in invitation.

She couldn't *not* lie down beside him. He was very conscious of the healing wounds, and she was open to his vulnerability. Laura sat down by him to stretch and yawned. Then she told him. "You ought to be in shorts."

"I will be soon." His thigh was appalling. He decided he would let her get used to the lesser scarring on his body and left arm first. Then he would expose the leg.

"This is a work of art for a surgeon." She lightly traced the curving incision that had allowed them to repair his arm. "As an artist, I can also appreciate how the doctor cut along the clearest path to do the least additional harm. When it fades, you'll appreciate it more."

He thought if she could see his injuries in that way, she could probably handle seeing his thigh.

With the same interest, she looked at his chest where the tear had been from the splintered steering wheel and the dashboard. It wasn't as artful, but the salvaging was ingenious. "Have you really looked at this?" she asked. "Obviously, it's your stomach, so you must have. See how this tear was repaired? Patched. Clever. You lucked in to a genius. Was the doctor someone you knew?"

"Pot luck. She happened to be there in the hospital."

"You have a guardian angel."

"I begin to believe it."

She leaned down and gently kissed his healing wounds. "I'm glad you survived."

"Me too."

She moved away to lie down beside him.

"Laura..." He turned onto his left, scarred side concealing it from her. "I can't believe you're here. I've dreamed it so many times, that I would turn over and find you beside me, that I can't believe it's true and you're here."

"Oh, Tanner..."

"I want you."

"It scares me a little."

"Don't be afraid of me," he urged.

"Not of you. Of me. I'm not sure whether this attraction is really 'love' or simply intense desire. I'm boggled by sensation when I'm around you. And I'm not sure I'm ready to be distracted from my own life. I've only just begun to learn independence. It's a heady feeling to run my own business, to have all the decisions and responsibility and for it to be successful. To be in control of my life. I went from father to the university to husband. I've just started to explore a business potential that's endless. It's exciting. And I'm good. I . . . hesitate to be distracted from it.''

"Do you find me distracting?" His voice was husky and he lifted his good right arm so his fingers could move a strand of hair from her face.

"You're really smooth, Tanner. Why do I suspect you're trying to lull me into a seduction?"

"Never." She watched his lazy smile as he explained, "I'm only showing you I'm interested, and willing."

"You believe I'll seduce you?"

"I wouldn't struggle." His smile turned quite wicked. "I don't believe I've ever thanked you properly for helping clean up the kitchen." He leaned over and kissed her. When he raised his head she could see his blue eyes were vulnerable with desire and shaded by his surprising lashes. He smiled a little.

She gasped and he kissed her again. Her hands were in his thick hair and her back arched as she pressed her breasts to his chest. His hand slid into the conveniently accessible wraparound dress, and his strong fingers closed around the taut mound of her breast. She made a soft sound in her throat, and his chest rumbled in a very pleased male sound.

She recognized the volcanic urgency in that sound. His passion rumbled there ready to explode, but she wasn't yet really ready for the consequences of what would happen if she made love with Tanner. She drew back. He protested and frowned, and his hands resisted her leaving him. It would have been very easy to simply allow him to convince her to stay there with him. To lie with him on that double lounger in the soft air with the sea breeze—and they would make love. She wanted him very badly. She could have him. It was her choice.

However she rose from the lounger and, gathering her scattered wits, she managed to say quite primly, "I believe the best thing for me to do, under the circumstances, is go for a good long run on the beach. Too bad you can't, too. But the time will come when you're stronger and then you can chase me."

He'd raised one knee and propped his foot to keep it there, as he put his hands behind his head to lie there watching her. How could blue eyes look so hot? He made his voice curl through her nervous system as he inquired, "When I can run, you'll let me chase you?"

"Perhaps." She gave him a sassy look.

"It'll be an incentive to work at my recovery." He made the words a threatening promise that did strange things to her beleaguered innards.

She went up to her room in order to change into the purple shorts. Although she made a concerted search, she could find no shoes that fit well enough and that wouldn't risk blisters. She decided to run barefooted on the water-packed sand at the tide's edge.

When she left her room to go down the stairs again, Laura found Tanner leaning casually on his crutch as he waited for her at the bottom of the stairs. He was a very strong presence. She smiled a little, and his return smile was like a predator's watching his victim. His eyes were like a hunter's. He looked excessively dangerous. To a woman. She felt a thrill go through her body and curl in her stomach. She wanted him to pursue her. And ... to catch her.

He said, as if it was natural, "You need to kiss me goodbye."

"I thought the kisses were just for good-night?"

"And goodbyes," he corrected the rules.

She lifted her brows a little as she tilted back her head, but she couldn't prevent the slightest little smile.

He intoned, elaborating, "Today we also kiss goodbye ... and then hello."

"I hadn't realized that. When was the decision made?"

"It was there all along. So you might just as well get it over with." He moved a step toward her in order to help her.

"I suppose I might just as well." She heaved a big, enduring sigh and met him halfway. She raised her mouth and closed her eyes.

Nothing happened. She peeked and he was watching her very seriously. She opened her eyes all the way and looked up at him. She too became serious. She slid her hands up his chest and around his shoulders to the back of his head, then she met his lips and she kissed him.

It was a stunning kiss. His arms went around her body and he pulled her to him hungrily. His kiss was deep and intense, and his reaction was passionate as he reveled in the feel of her against him, the sensations she aroused in him. The thrill of her. Her hands petting the back of his head, her body so soft and feminine against his, her sweet mouth kissing him back. He finally lifted his head to gasp air and groaned before he looked down at her with a rueful smile. "Scat! Go while you can."

It was a commentary on her condition that she obeyed him. She wasn't in control of her own mind, and she accepted his direction. She almost staggered to the front door, fumbled with the latch, practically fell out onto the porch and made it to the top of the steps.

He watched with smoldering, pleased eyes as she stood on the porch and breathed deeply, in order to orient herself. She pushed her hair back several times, although the wind was already doing that for her, and she looked around as if trying to remember why she was there on the porch.

Running? her body asked. Running was the last thing it wanted to do. It wanted to go right back to Tanner and experience all those promises his kisses offered. Why had she decided to run? While she was trying to figure out why she was outside, her mind directed that she go on down the steps and across the deserted road. She automatically remembered to look for traffic before she crossed, even though there was never any traffic out there. She slipped out of the thongs, and did some warm-ups before she slowly jogged off up the beach.

Since she wasn't used to the endlessness or the sameness of deserted beaches as opposed to city blocks or tracks she went too far. So she was a long time coming back. Tanner found her tiredly returning, as he drove along the shore road searching for her. She fell into the car gratefully. This car was another Porsche to replace the wrecked one.

"You have to set a landmark," Tanner explained. He didn't scold her or mention how anxious he'd become when she was gone for so long. "That way you judge how far you'll go and remember you have to come back the same distance."

"Glad you mentioned it." She was lying back, really exhausted, sipping a can of orange juice he'd brought along for her.

They drove in silence. Laura became relaxed and contented. Tanner was still coping with his uneasiness over her long absence.

She broke the silence to tell him, "Look for the dog."

He slowed, frowning, seeing no dog. "What dog?"

"I think someone threw him out or he's lost. A black dog, like a Scottish Collie. No tags. Not frisky. I'm afraid of dogs so I didn't examine him closely. But there're no houses in sight around here. He didn't look like he was adventuring but just waiting by the road."

"We'll watch."

They were silent as they looked. The longer it took, the slower he drove, and they were all the way back to his house and hadn't seen the dog. "I suppose he went on home?" she suggested uncertainly.

"Let's go take another look." He swung into the drive in order to turn around.

"Oh, Tanner..." Her smile melted his heart and he leaned to kiss her. As he lifted his mouth, she asked, "Is that the hello one?"

"No, that's an I'm-on-your-side one."

"It felt like a hello one."

"You've still got that one to anticipate."

"Oh, I suppose..." But she smiled and her eyes were warm.

They had to go back and forth still another time before they found the dog. He was curled up out of the wind in a slight depression so he could watch the road. In the darkness of the depression his black coat seemed only like a deeper shadow.

They had a tough time coaxing the dog into the car. He watched along the road one last time before he slowly climbed into the back seat and carefully sat down. His eyes were dulled but intelligent.

"Is it sick?" she asked in concern.

"I think he's only hungry. We'll take him on over to Henry the vet right now and have him looked at. Poor mutt."

The veterinarian's office was in an old farmhouse. There were pens for dogs and a goat. Two horses came to a fence to see who was there and there was a world of cats.

Henry squatted down and talked to the dog first. The dog was a little anxious and was looking around. They gave him water, and the dog lapped it up. Then Henry gave him a little dry food. The dog was starved.

Henry told them, "I can see no injuries. There's nothing to identify him, just the flea collar and that's new, oddly enough. Good thing. This is supposed to be the Year of the Flea. His coat isn't too bad, his teeth are all there. He's a young dog. Beautiful animal. It kills my heart, people think animals can survive on their own in the country. He could be lost but there's been no notice about such a dog running loose around here. I'll inquire around. Thanks for bringing him in. He'll find a home."

Tanner and Laura turned slowly away but as they started to get into the Porsche, the dog made a sound in his throat. Not a whimper or anything begging. Just a questioning. They both turned back.

Quite cheerfully Henry said, "We'll give him the shots and you can take him along." And he grinned at the pair.

Tanner looked at Laura. "We have a dog?"

Five

They took the dog back to the Moran beach house and, with the April day bright and warm, they bathed him outside. He stood obediently for their convenience and he didn't appear to mind the water. Tanner took off his shirt, unselfconscious now about his healing body, and he first rinsed off the dog.

Laura held the hose and kept her distance while Tanner soaped the patient animal. "He's charming. I never thought I'd say that about a dog."

"Someone must have lost him. No one would throw away such a dog."

"He always turns to face the road," Laura commented.

"Yes."

"Tanner, neither of us has the time nor the place for a dog. This interlude is unfair for him. He could become attached to us and then have to go on to someone else. He's obviously loyal. He's looking for people in a car to come back for him."

To soothe her worry, he told her, "When school's out in another month or so, this place is going to be overflowing with little cousins. Dog can choose a new attachment. I'd like to keep him in the family." With old towels Tanner began to rub the dog dry then brushed his coat. The dog held still for it. "What'll we name him?"

"I'm not sure we should," Laura replied thoughtfully. "What if the next person who has him wants another name? It's asking a lot for a dog to remember changing labels."

"We could call him Dog. That way it won't be a name but it's still a label."

And just then as if responding to canine labeling, Pam came around from the front of the house. She was beautifully dressed in a dinner dress and heels, and her hair was perfectly done. She paused as she saw Laura, and asked abruptly, "You're still here?"

Laura didn't know how to reply to that. Obviously she was still there.

Tanner said, "Hello, Pam, want a dog?"

"Oh, Tanner!" she exclaimed in shock. "Ugh! Put your shirt on!" And she covered her eyes.

He looked blank for half a pause before he said, "Of course." And he slipped into the shirt to screen his healing body. "It's okay now."

"That's better." Pam then looked at Tanner. "I thought we could go into town for dinner tonight."

"I'm sorry." He smiled at her. "We have plans. Thanks for asking us."

She gave Laura a cold look that should have shriveled her, and after a mouth-working frustrating minute, she left.

They didn't say anything for a while. It had been a strange intrusion. Then Tanner said, "It's interesting to see Pam under these circumstances—with you here. I'd never have dreamed she could be so rude to you. How can she be as old as she is and so unthinking about my scars?"

"I've had the advantage of working with people who've had either horrendous injuries or surgery. Both men and women have a tough time dealing with disfigurement, even if it's only temporary. Pam probably doesn't think about you being scarred, she relates it to herself, and how she'd feel if it was she who had those injuries. She really didn't mean to be nasty to you."

"How can you defend her?" He stopped brushing the dog to look at Laura, as he waited for her reply.

"Rather grudgingly. I don't like her, but she wants you. That shows she has superb taste."

"Granted."

"And in my sojourn on this planet..."

"Sojourn?" He grinned at her word.

"I'm an observer and a firm believer in reincarnation. And in this particular life, I've learned that rude people are unhappy. I can endure them for the brief time I must, but they have to live with themselves all the time. No relief. That's burden enough."

"I like you."

Laura smiled as she watched Tanner's big hard hands on the dog. "You're so gentle."

"He's been weather worn and hungry. His skin is probably a little tender. His feet are sand roughened. I have some oil Henry gave me. In a few days he'll feel well and strong again."

"I just hope some of the kids get a chance at him." She caught his eye and smiled, teasing him.

How strange that a man could be so gentle, especially one who lived such a rootless, potentially dangerous life as Tanner. He was really a very tender man. The way he'd searched for the lost dog, and cared for it now, seeing to its health and comfort proved that. "Why did you choose the particular work you do?" Laura surprised herself with the strange change of subject.

"I'm a civilized man."

She laughed. "Hunting crooks is civilized?"

"Absolutely. I'm for law and order and the rights of individuals to be treated honestly and fairly."

She waited but he added nothing more. Then she examined his words and found he'd explained civilization quite adequately. Impulsively she said, "I love you, Tanner."

He smiled but his eyes were on the dog. "I know you do."

"I've only been here two days, and I've slept upstairs out of reach. How could you think I love you?"

"Love is more than just sex," he told her complacently. "You stayed with me. You came here, and you didn't want to leave. You aren't all the way committed to me yet, but you're considering it. You're a little afraid of it. I believe you consider a commitment as similar to a sacrificial maiden being coaxed to fling herself into an active volcano." He turned his head to grin up at her, but he kept on gently brushing the dog.

"An active volcano?" She considered the comparison. "That's really very close."

"I've never known anyone who kissed in such an abandoned, committed way. You lift my hair right off my scalp. You do some other interesting things to me too."

She scoffed, "I think you're just susceptible."

"To you."

"Do you feel this amazing pull between us, too? I've never felt it with anyone else. I get in the same room with you and it's almost frightening."

"Don't be afraid of me, Laura."

"I would bet they said that to all the sacrificial maidens." She frowned as she said, "If you are equated to a volcano, for Pete's sake, how do you survive?"

"Not at all well. I need my fires banked and tended."

The most surprising wave of sensation washed over Laura. It went through every cell and nerve and tingled so that she was astonished her atoms didn't become confused and fly off in all directions. Impulsively, she asked, "Did you read that we're not solid but just clusters of atoms that are magnetically attracted?"

He chuckled. "Now whatever made you think of that?"

"*My* atoms are vibrating."

"That's serious. I hope I'm involved when they explode."

"It could blow up the volcano," she said seriously.

He glanced up and she could see the fires in the core of the inferno. "I would risk it gladly."

She watched him stand and knew he was going to come to her and take her into his arms. Vibrating, about to come unglued, she waited.

He looked at his watch. "What with you running away from home and our searching out and taking care of Dog here, it's supper time. Want to go into Myrtle Beach and have some sea food?"

Food? He could think of food *now*? How irritating! With barely throttled sarcasm, she exclaimed, "Perfect! I can wear my own clothes for a change." She hopped up and started for the house. But she hadn't taken five steps before she stopped to turn back. "What about Dog?"

"He knows he can stay here. He can be on the front porch. I'll put his food and water and an old rag rug there. That way he can watch the road."

And she had been irritated with him! She watched with some amazement as he picked up the hose and carried it back to turn it off and wind it on the brace. He'd left his crutch on the ground! "Tanner? You're walking without the crutch!" It was a miracle!

He grinned. "You're no longer afraid of me so I can get rid of the damned thing."

"Do you mean...? You snookered me!"

"That sounds about right. I didn't want you to feel threatened. I figured if you thought I couldn't chase you or climb stairs, you'd feel more in control and safer out here all alone with me in the wilds of the South Carolina coast."

"And you claim to be civilized! You sneak!" she sputtered. "You pirate! You trickster!"

"None of the above." He was good-humored. "I'm calculating and clever. I fully intended to tell you about it because I thought of it! It was brilliant! Pete called and said you were coming down...."

"He told me he would only say a proxy was going to visit you for him."

"He lied. He told me it would be you. I had only a few hours of intense plotting to figure out how to keep you here. If you hadn't agreed to stay, I was going to become disabled."

"Disabled?"

He confessed readily enough, "I was going to wing that one. Either be sick or fall—nothing too drastic— but not be able to take care of myself. That way your tender heart would have been touched..."

"Well, darn. I wish I hadn't leaped at the offer. Now I'll never know how you would have manipulated me. Just witnessing your performance would have been worth the time."

He wasn't that sure. "As I said, I'm not at all good at acting. I've never had to."

"Just snapped your fingers?"

"No, I never wanted to entrance any other woman as I want you."

"I'm a little scared."

"You unsettle me a little too."

"So." She put her hand to her chest and took a steadying breath. "So you can walk unaided."

"I can't run yet. Honest. I can't even jog yet. Stairs are still tricky, even without suitcases. But I do walk on the beach. I went almost as far as you did when I walked last night."

"But you didn't see Dog?"

"I wasn't looking for anything. I was walking and trying to calm down from that crippling good-night kiss you gave me. He probably watched me go past, tearing my hair and gnashing my teeth in frustration."

Heartlessly, she thought he was being amusing.

* * *

They drove into Myrtle Beach. It was still crowded with the seasonal invasion of Canadians and braced for the onslaught of college kids who came there on spring break. At one of the excellent restaurants on Ocean Boulevard they ate dinner and had a very pleasant evening. They spent almost three hours on good food and conversation. They remembered, they discussed, they laughed. They exchanged bites of their foods. And after the evening was over, they went back to the waiting house.

Dog was still on the porch. He got up and trotted after the Porsche as it went around the house. When the car stopped, Dog came to stand and watch them in a friendly way as they left the car. They both spoke to the dog. Tanner petted him, but Laura still kept her distance.

Leaving the dog to go back to his vigil, they went into the house. Tanner immediately went to the kitchen sink and washed his hands quite carefully. To Laura it seemed a curious thing to do. As he reached for a towel, he saw that she watched and he explained, "When I get my good-night kiss, I want to smell you, not Dog."

"After his bath he probably smells like a rose."

"Not exactly. Not bad, but still like a dog. He's a grown male." He swung his head around and smiled faintly. "And so am I."

"Don't frighten me."

"I never would."

"I'll bet you're leading up to the good-night kiss?"

"Inevitably." He seemed quite serious as he dried his hands.

The single word started her nerves shimmering. Her breathing faltered. With her hot breath pouring over her lips they would be like sandpaper when he finally got around to kissing her! She licked her lips hastily.

He kissed her just like the night before. He kissed her hands first, rather pointedly, and then he took her into his arms and hugged her so deliciously that her brain swooned. Then he really kissed her. Beautifully. He melted her bones and set her blood afire. He ruined her respiratory system entirely. After all those years, her lungs forgot how to function. It was chaos.

Then he pried her away from him and smiled sweetly as he said good-night. And again he patted her bottom in that sassy way as he started her up the stairs. How could he abandon her? She went up the stairs debating taking off her clothes as she walked back down to him. He was standing there watching her. What would he do?

He might allow her to seduce him. But then again he could very well fetch her a robe and send her back upstairs again. He wasn't predictable. Imagine his pretending to need a crutch in order to keep her from feeling threatened. It wasn't him she worried about. It was herself!

She wanted him. She wanted to lie in his arms and have him make love to her. It would be so...nice. But he was thinking long term and she was thinking greedy. Wasn't it generally the other way around? Was she the victim of role reversal? Was this what the columnists were talking about?

She'd always been told to behave. Especially if she cared for a man. The saying was that a woman is a prude until she loves a man, then she has the morals of an alley cat; while a man will take anything offered until he loves a woman, then he's pure as the driven snow.

Perhaps that's what the trouble really was. The hang-up wasn't role reversal, but the male-female confrontation that was old as time. They loved each other and were reacting typically. Nothing was new. It was the same old thing. And she'd been as guilty as had every other generation in thinking anything was different.

So he was waiting for her commitment. He was giving her time to know him. To be sure he loved her, but how well could she love him? That was an important question. She was most assuredly attracted. God knew that. She had always been drawn to Tanner. He was so superb, so special and so attractive.

Bemused she went about the automatic routine of preparing for bed. She heard without hearing, the surf, the wind in the palms, the house shifting, the car drive by and... A car? It was probably the first she'd heard since she came there! How amazing. Civilization did exist.

She gazed at herself in the mirror, and decided she looked like a klutz. Pigtails, T-shirt and panties. Old cotton panties with loose elastic. What a dream woman.

What if he came up the stairs to say good-night again? What if he decided to coax her into taking a sample of Tanner's other talents? He'd take one look at her and forget it.

She peeled off the T-shirt and panties and took out a slip that was navy blue and made mostly of lace. She considered it as a nightgown. It would have to do. She unbraided her hair and brushed it back into silkiness. She added a little eye shadow and then just a touch of blush.

She smiled into the mirror and pursed her lips in a phantom kiss. Not too tacky. She swaggered a little as she went over, eased down and wiggled between the sheets. She was ready.

She went to sleep listening for him on the stairs.

With dawn she found herself wrapped in the sheet with her slip wound around her so uncomfortably that she was reminded why she slept in T-shirt and old panties. She lay there, irritated, thinking disgruntled thoughts at Tanner.

Why blame him? she thought. What if she wasn't interested? What if he came up the stairs to try her and she didn't want to? There they were, out here all alone, in the middle of nowhere. If he tried to rape her what could she do about it? If she hadn't wanted him, why was she staying there alone with him? The rules of

convention were good practical rules that simply had
to be observed.

But she *was* willing. That was what surprised her so
much when she had agreed to stay there with Tanner.
The only man she'd ever slept with had been Tom. She
had never cared much for Tom's lovemaking and
therefore had never been tempted to try another
man...until now. She was now willing. It was Tanner who was being obtuse. She would simply have to
indicate that he had a free hand, so to speak. She
smiled.

How does a woman go about a seduction? she
thought. A good meal, low lights, sexy gown, loose
shoulder strap. Right. She would seduce him. That
decided so handily, she got out of bed and unwound
her slip so she could remove it. Then she looked over
her clothes. Obviously she'd not packed with seduction in mind.

She went into the hall and checked through the guest
closet. There was a fascinating collection of odds and
ends of clothing, and she found a cigar box with an
assortment of costume jewelry. It was the type gathered for children to use while playing dress-up on rainy
days. But nowhere in that practical closet was there
anything near to what she was looking for in seduc-
tive clothing. A bikini that was a little tired looking
was about the only thing that came even close, but the
Atlantic in April tended to be quite cold. So, that
eliminated the excuse to wear even the tired bikini. It
was apparent that seduction could be a problem.

She heard a truck drive up. Last night she'd heard a car, today a truck. It was time to move on west. Civilization was intruding. Long ago, a pioneer in Indiana had moved west because someone homesteaded twelve miles from him, crowding him.

She put on the wraparound and thongs and went downstairs. Two men were delivering boxes into her morning room. Well, she hadn't needed the entire room, she told herself, but it still seemed intrusive of Tanner to put the boxes there when other rooms weren't being used.

She went into the kitchen and saw the grill on top of the stove and pancake batter ready nearby. The way she was eating, she would have to find some more wraparounds.

After setting the table she worked at making their meal. She listened to Tanner's deep voice as he spoke to the delivery men. When Tanner realized he was being seduced would his deep voice tremble and squeak? Well, she'd soon find out!

Within that creaking house on a palm-studded sea coast, she felt a little like a woman pirate. Ho ho ho and a bottle of rum. Rum! *That* was the other missing ingredient to seduction. Candy's dandy but liquor's quicker. How could she have forgotten?

Tanner came into the kitchen as the laboring sound of the delivery truck faded away, and he found Laura up on her Cratchit stool with her head in an upper cupboard. "What are you doing?" he asked her.

"I'm studying your liquor cellar for rum."

"For *breakfast*?" He seemed surprised.

She pulled her head out of the cupboard and gave him a slow, enigmatic smile. "You've never had rum in your pancake syrup?"

"I don't believe so," he replied unsurprisingly.

"Let's live a little."

"I have a surprise for you."

Her smile crept back salaciously, "Ah, and I have one for you!"

"Do I get it now or after breakfast?" He gave her the choice.

"After. Everything's ready so let's eat first." She smiled still. Once they got in bed, they might miss several meals. She thought he appeared...a little stimulated. Did he suspect she planned to seduce him? He seemed anxious to get through breakfast, and they ate with very little conversation. He was nice about the rum-soaked pancakes and agreed they were different. She smiled at him and made her eyelids heavy.

Tanner had studied her through breakfast, trying to figure her out. She acted a little drunk. On rum-soaked pancakes? Curious. Nevertheless, he hurried her along. He was anxious to see her reaction to the things he'd ordered.

She insisted on clearing up the kitchen. There was nothing more depressing than to return to a kitchen and find the ruins of a meal waiting to be dealt with. She quickly hurried the mess out of the way. "Was Dog fed?"

"Long ago, sleepyhead."

"He's still around?"

He nodded. "On the porch, watching."

"I thought maybe the car last night—"

"Car? You heard a car? When?"

"Yeah. When I was getting ready for bed. I think we ought to move on west, partner, it's getting crowded around these parts."

"What kind of car?" He frowned and his question was quickly asked.

"I didn't see it, I just heard it! It's a public road, you know. I thought it might be Dog's people come back for him."

"No."

He had become a little distracted from her. She went to him and put her arms around his shoulders and lifted her mouth. "Good morning."

"You train well. I am pleased." He kissed her sputtering mouth and he laughed.

"Train . . . !" she began indignantly.

But he only patted her bottom and said, "Come see."

He led her into the morning room and immediately began to open the boxes. He clamped the holder for the butcher paper on one end of the drafting table, and found the giant roll of paper it would take a year to use up, if she worked at it diligently. Artists use butcher paper in many ways, as a cover to prevent smears, as scratch paper, as a clean surface, as a paint tester. It is marvelously versatile.

Then he put out the brushes. Beautiful sable ones, from a brush of a single hair to a Japanese hand brush to one to paint huge ink letters on paper and on cloth. He went to the kitchen for pots and crocks and set the brushes in them on end. His generosity boggled her mind and twisted her tongue so that she could only stare with her mouth open and itch to try them all.

All those inks and paints! With such an inventory, she could start classes! Then he opened the boxes. There were swatches of material, from Damask to the finest silks, from burlaps to linen. Laura was overwhelmed. She started to laugh and cry.

"Are you pleased?"

"Oh, Tanner..." How could she tell him she was crying because if she seduced him now, he would think it was in gratitude for gifts.

"I think then, that you could kiss me for a thank-you, don't you?"

"Oh, Tanner..." And she flung herself into his arms and hugged him for a long time, which he permitted. And then she kissed him very sweetly, which he also permitted. He cooperated, and she could have snatched him bald for causing the delay of his seduction! Another night in that bed alone.

The weather continued its taste of summer for several more days. Laura and Tanner breakfasted together, then separated to their workrooms until lunch and walked along the beach in the afternoons. Dog sat on the porch or roamed along the road, but he walked along the beach with them as he watched the road.

And they kissed. Every day Tanner added more reasons for kisses. And Laura agreed readily and cooperated with an eagerness that spun his head around. He smiled to himself and thought it wouldn't be long before he had her.

In her turn, Laura also plotted. How interesting that they were each so involved in the other's seduction they couldn't pay attention and realize what was going on and work together.

Being her thrifty mother's child, and one of four daughters, Laura could sew. She chose a swatch of blues and lavenders in lovely swirls. Using an elderly machine she found in the upstairs sewing room, she made herself a dress. A dress for a seduction. It turned out very sweet. It wasn't at all sexy. Disgruntled, she put it aside. She wanted something to curl his toes.

She again went through the swatches and found a fiery red. Men like red. It was almost as clingy as a parachute silk. It was horrible to work with, and she grimly finished it. It was perfect. She did look a little like a street walker, but at least there was no question. She didn't look unavailable. She was ready.

The red dress demanded some adornment besides the pearl buttons she wore in her ears and sudden inspiration sent her back to the guest closet where she went through the box of old jewelry. There were lots of beads, some bracelets. But mostly single, clip-on earrings.

One earring was a white rhinestone cluster with only two stones missing. It also had strings of rhinestones hanging in a bunch. It was, of course, a singleton. She found another that was also made of white rhinestones mixed with a pinky violet that went quite well with the red. It, too, hung to her shoulder. She would wear them with the dress. They looked like something a loose woman would wear.

That made her wonder a little about how the earrings had come to be in that house? It had probably been the woman whose "ghost" she'd heard on that first night. She'd had a rather knowing laugh.

So she had the perfect dress and earrings. She was ready. However, after two concentrated days of furious sewing she was tired, cross and had a headache. The weather was turning sullen and gray. She'd really pushed it by making two dresses in two days. It was no time to try for a seduction, she'd probably snap at him and ruin everything and then cry in disappointment, and he'd turn her out of the house.

With the weather muggy and still, she took her headache down to the kitchen to go through the freezer. Being on the coast, there were shrimp in plenty. There was also frozen lobster bisque, some shrimp creole and long slender loaves of bread. He should be pleased she didn't have to cook it herself. She wasn't that imaginative nor was she any kind of cook.

She thawed a large container of stew and a loaf of Vienna bread for their supper. Then she added a

Mountain Top pumpkin pie. Let Pam eat her heart out.

Tanner was surprised to find supper ready. "How nice of you!"

"Do you think you're the only one who can thaw things?"

"You're my guest. I'm supposed to take care of you. You're working too hard. I shouldn't have gotten you all that stuff at once. I should have stretched it out over the summer."

"I can't stay here all summer." She was softly regretful.

"We'll see." He was dismissive to such a problem.

She explained, "All your family will be here in another month."

"They come in layers. They peak on the Fourth of July. We have a hell of a party then. It's fun. You'll have a good time, and they'll all love you." His eyes never left her.

"We do that on the Fourth at home, in South Bend."

"Are you feeling okay?" He was frowning at her.

"Fine."

"Let me feel your forehead." He laid his big, warm hand on her hot, blushing face.

"I'm fine, really. Just a little tired."

"I think you have a fever. You look a little too bright-eyed and flushed. I'll get the thermometer." He began to look through cupboards.

So she had a headache. All that was wrong with her was sexual frustration. Did he mistake thwarted passion for an illness? "You could take me over to the veterinarian like you did Dog," she suggested.

"I wouldn't let Henry touch you to examine you."

"Why not?"

"I change around you," he explained brusquely. "My teeth sharpen, my arms get long, my forehead slopes back sharply, my knuckles drag on the ground."

"Really? I hadn't noticed that. Why?"

"Didn't you see how he leered at you when we took Dog over there?"

"Henry acted perfectly normal. Friendly."

"See?"

"He was supposed to be rude?"

"Only professional." Tanner shook down the thermometer and poked it in her mouth.

Around it she said, "But you—"

"Be quiet."

She subsided. With the thermometer in her mouth she felt even more rotten. She had a cold? That would postpone the seduction of Tanner for another couple of days. She felt sour.

In broad humor, he asked, "Are you acting sick just so you can stay? How unoriginal of you. I'll allow you to stay without being sick."

"Good grief." The thermometer rattled between her teeth.

"Be quiet."

Six

She had no fever. He frowned at her bright eyes and reddened cheeks. He seemed so concerned that she explained herself to him, well enough, "I just need a Vitamin C and a Tylenol. I'll be fine. It's all this sea air." She was on a roll. "My lungs and blood aren't used to the salt. As a prairie woman, of pioneer stock, I'm genetically too many generations removed from the primal salt swamp. The readjusting takes a while."

"You need an early night. I didn't mean to overwhelm you with all that junk to sort through."

"Junk! Oh, Tanner, it was like having five Christmases at once. All those gorgeous things! I must at least share in the costs. The bill will be staggering."

"They're gifts. No true courtesan offers to pay…in money." He smiled.

"Oh? Compromising gifts? How shocking."

"At times your eyes are such an innocent blue and then there are times like these—with rum-soaked pancakes and with my suggestion you can trade your body for priceless gifts—and your eyes are very very wicked. My mother never mentioned women like you. She always told me to be kind."

"And what did your dad tell you?"

Tanner squinted his eyes for a minute, as he recalled, then he quoted, " 'Don't turn down anything until you check it out to see if it's worth it.' Hmmmm. Do you suppose he meant women? I always thought he meant stocks! He was an investor. Why, I do believe he misled me."

"You idiot."

"I believe I have been." He smiled. "Shall we cure your headache?"

Regretfully she said, "If my heartbeat went up even one more notch, my head would explode and that'd be a god-awful mess."

He nodded thoughtfully. "Might be a turnoff."

"Oh, Tanner, you are something else." She smiled at him.

Outside on the road, the sound of a car went past. Tanner simply disappeared. Vanished. She saw him and then he was gone! There had been no sound, nothing. She stood up, her eyes enormous, and she looked at the floor. She peeked into the center hall and then went into his study. Nothing.

She turned back to the hall and looked around, getting spooked. What if there was something strange about the house? What if there *wasn't* any family and he was the only surviving member and the house fed on the souls of strangers lured into...

And there he was in front of her!

She shrieked, and he looked very surprised. He reached for her and she backed away, saying a moaning, "Oh, no!"

He thought she'd flipped. "Laura?"

"Is it you, Tanner?"

"What did you see?"

What was there *to* see? She stared at him with huge, haunted eyes. "How'd you do that?"

"What?" he asked a little puzzled.

"Disappear like that."

He frowned, trying to understand, and told her, "I went to the front door to see what kind of car went by."

"Did you fly? There was no sound."

His face was blank, and then slowly a smile came into his eyes and his mouth quirked. "You think the house is haunted and I'm a spook." He nodded, very amused.

She agreed, "You didn't really survive the wreck. You weren't ready to depart this vale of tears."

"Ah. Am I a vampire?"

She frowned at him. "No. You do go out into the sun." That would tend to eliminate the vampire theory. "How did you vanish from the kitchen that way?"

He became serious, knowing now that she was, too. He took her arms and moved her to one side. He went to the kitchen and dashed out, past her and to the front door. He made no sound at all. She had followed him and they stood there in the soft darkness.

"I thought you couldn't run."

"I didn't. I only hurried."

It was true. "Are you real, Tanner?"

"Painfully so." He watched her.

"Did you ever read about the Englishman a hundred or so years ago who said he could run between two towns and there were bets for and against him, and a carriage of witnesses went along to see there was no cheating, and he appeared to stumble on the bare roadway and he simply vanished. They never did find him."

"You thought I was gone?"

"It scared me."

"If I left I'd take you with me." He took hold of her upper arms, his strong hands didn't hurt her, but he held her very firmly. "Your time has come, Laura Fullerton. Face it bravely." His voice was low and husky.

"Tanner..."

He kissed her. Beautifully. Marvelously. Then he slung her over one hip to carry her awkwardly with only his good right arm, and his limp became pronounced.

"You can't do this. I'm too heavy."

"I am doing it." He was struggling along.

"This is ridiculous."

"It's romantic," he corrected. "I want our first time to be romantic."

"You're ruining my stomach."

"I'll soothe it in just a minute."

"You're not going to try for the stairs are you?" she asked in alarm.

With a bit of uncertainty he replied, "Well...if you really prefer to be on your own bed..."

"No no no. Why are we going anywhere? What was wrong with the rug in the front room?"

"I would hate for our grandchildren to gossip about their grandmother's first time being on the floor, and their grandfather being so greedy that he couldn't sweep grandmaw up in his arms and carry her to a decent couch at the very least. A bed sounds a little too deliberate, don't you agree? Not at all impulsive but more calculated."

"Grandchildren?"

"I'm going to marry you, Scarlett honey. I can't keep waiting to catch you between husbands. One might live."

"I was divorced," she said in a record-keeping way, then she asked, "Scarlett honey? You read GWTW?"

He paused as if to consider, but he was really catching his breath. "GWTW? Ahhh, of course, *Gone*

With the Wind. Why naturally I read it. All the women go bonkers over Rhett, so I had to plow through a couple of thousand pages to see what turned them all so eager. All I could find out was that he kept trying to get Scarlett into bed. Now *that's* something *I* could do!''

Quite pensive, she told him, "I've always wanted to make love with you."

"You could have mentioned it." He sounded a little annoyed.

"I didn't realize that was what it was until you kissed me in the receiving line when Tom and I were married."

"It was a little late by then."

"Yes. I've thought about you a time or two."

"Me, too."

"You ought to put me down," she suggested. "You're ruining your lungs trying to carry me along this way."

"It isn't carrying you that's ruining my lungs, it's your soft body against mine and me knowing I'm going to make love to you."

"This must be killing your arm."

"You may have gained a bit."

"I haven't either!"

He leaned an arm against the wall to rest, but he still held her over his good hip. "You have the most gorgeous hips."

"You haven't even looked at my hips. I was watching."

"I've made a concerted study of you. I know your hips in detail, if you'll pardon the expression."

"Put me down, Tanner."

"I've offended you? Most women wouldn't mind if—"

"I can't wait any longer."

"Here on the floor? My God, Scarlett. What will our grandchildren say to that? Shocking. Shocking." But he put her down. He was trembling and as he kissed her his breath was harsh.

"See? You've exhausted yourself! You won't have the energy to even—"

"Don't worry."

"I can't have you ruin yourself just to satisfy me."

He laughed with such amusement. "Laura, baby, don't you worry. I'm fine. Or almost. I will be pretty soon now. Kiss me."

But she went on fretting. "You're trembling. Your muscles are—"

"It isn't exhaustion, it's desire." His voice was gruff, but amusement laced his words.

"Really? Tom never... I didn't know. I thought... Tanner. Oh, Tanner."

"I do like wraparounds. Oh, my love." He drew in his breath as he opened her gown and surveyed her body in the soft light. Then he slid the garment off her shoulders to the floor.

"Let me help you." She reached for him.

But he moved away. "Let's go over here into the dark." He still hadn't exposed his left thigh to her eyes. Very quickly to get past it, he told her, "Don't move your right leg against my left thigh. That's the only thing. You can do anything else you want to, but just watch the left thigh."

"I love you."

"Marry me."

"We'll talk about it."

"Now, Laura, just..."

"Kiss me, Tanner."

"We..."

She kissed him lovingly and he cooperated quite nicely. She breathed, "Oh, Tanner..." Then she undid his trousers very boldly, surprising them both. She knelt to slide the soft material off his legs and it was then she saw the night-shadowed wounds in his thigh. Very softly, she ran her hand over his healing leg in an accepting caress. She filled his heart and he drew in his breath as he watched her fingers slide higher. She murmured, "You are so beautiful."

And he looked down at her, kneeling before him, and his voice was unsteady with emotion as he said, "Laura!" in a passionate whisper.

Before then, she hadn't thought how abrasive even so soft a rug might be on his wounds. She led him to his bed and lay so he could be on his good right side as they began their explorations. Their appreciation of each other.

They kissed almost as if to consume, their hands searching, their fingers stiffened with their desire. With the fire that burned in them. She made little squeaking sounds and tears slid from her eyes, her emotion ran so high. So overwhelming. He was there in her arms!

He had planned to be tender and loving, but he was swept up in her passion and they spiraled far beyond anything either of them had ever experienced. It was out of control. They could only helplessly ride it out, frantically holding on, disoriented, plunging recklessly into another world. A place of thrilling sensations that obliterated all else.

After some time, their sated bodies lay as contented victims on his bed, there in the soft darkness. They could hardly move. They carefully turned their heads to smile at each other. But it was a little while before they were able to touch and clasp their hands. It was even longer before they spoke. At first they made only sounds. Sounds of pleasure.

"I never dreamed it would be like this." His voice was a rumble.

"I thought I was hallucinating. Is this some kind of psychedelic drug that's habit forming?"

"Whatever it is, I'm sure it's habit forming. I want more."

"You jest," she protested.

"Well, I didn't mean right this minute."

"I couldn't wiggle a muscle if my life depended on it."

"Oh, yes. Want me to show you that you could?"

"Don't threaten me."

"If I could move my arm and that hand," he promised. "I would prove you could move."

"I'll wait. Don't push yourself."

"You're the other half of me."

"I sure was," she agreed easily to that.

"I mean, we're meant to be."

"You are awesome." Her voice wasn't more than a whisper. "It was a little scary."

"Another dimension."

"Ummmm."

"You're so sweet and soft. You are such a lady and such a surprise in passion. I'm stunned. I wish I had the energy to see if it was really true."

"Not right away."

With some lazy effort he leaned up on his elbow to look down at her. He smiled into her eyes and gently kissed her swollen lips. "You look like you've been very very friendly with some willing man."

"How strange." Her eyes were sleepy and heavy lidded.

"Who was the lucky guy?"

"Some handsome stranger I ran into in the center hall who appears and vanishes."

"How's the headache?" He smoothed back her hair from her forehead.

"I have no idea. I believe I'm splattered somewhere in the marvelous inner space of fantastic colors. I feel so boneless and melted. What in the world did you do to me?"

"That was a restrained application of Tanner Moran's simple headache remedy. If you are a satisfied customer you owe me payment."

"What sort of payment?" She swiveled her head on his chest and her silken hair felt erotic to him even then when he was sated.

"I'll think of something."

"Not right away."

He laughed softly, lay back down beside her and held her hand curled in his. "The sheets are damp from your sweat."

"I never sweat."

"It couldn't be mine, I'm never sweaty or excited, either. I'm always calm and in control."

"Oh, yes?" She laughed softly.

"Well, perhaps a little 'excited' got in there somewhere tonight."

"Just a little?"

"You are fabulous."

"So are you."

"You are more than I."

They debated that and then each told how much the other was loved, how gorgeous each was and how sweet. And they argued who was more passionate, and eventually they had to prove their words. And they made sweet tender love that was entirely different but no less beautiful. And they smiled as they slid into peaceful sleep.

Neither heard the car drive by, but Dog watched it pass.

* * *

When Laura wakened to the birds' chatter it was to find Tanner propped on one elbow watching her. He had a knee over hers and one hand moved sensuously over her pleasured stomach. He smiled at her. She laughed.

"You find it amusing to wake up in my bed? When I've told you what all you did to me, you'll find it hilarious."

With great, droll humor, she informed him, "Upstairs, in my closet, is a red dress of asininely soft silk that clings like a second skin. I made it for your seduction tonight. And in the freezer is shrimp, lobster bisque and a shrimp creole to lure you into a good humor so that I can *coax* you into submitting to my carnal desires."

"I jumped the gun."

"Somewhat," she agreed.

"I'll wipe that from my mind...." But he had to put back his head and just laugh over how impossible that would be. "Well, what I can do is, I can pretend I've wiped it from my mind and your seduction can go along as scheduled. I can hardly wait."

"Oh, no," she said airily. "The element of surprise is ruined. I'll have to just forget it."

"Hey! I insist. Surprise me tonight with a full-out, calculated seduction. I'll behave."

Spacing her words with deliberate drollness, she instructed: "The purpose of a seduction, you idiot, is to get you *not* to behave."

"I hadn't realized that."

"I think initiating men is one of the most difficult things a woman must cope with."

"I need some lessons?" He couldn't even hold his voice steady. He knew how good he was.

"In some of the finer nuances. I believe in time, and with practice, you could be quite adequate." She lifted her brows and gave him a cool glance.

Deliberately he leaned over and his kiss was cunning. He changed the kiss and introduced his tongue into play, touching her lips and teasing hers into an assault of her mouth so that her tongue then touched his tauntingly as she resisted his intrusion. His hands moved, one stroking her susceptible stomach, which caused her breasts to rise, wanting attention. He lowered his mouth to them, and she began to breathe brokenly.

His own breath changed. It scorched along on her cool skin and his tongue was scalding. His muscles hardened, and his hot hands were a little rougher as his mouth nipped along her throat and began to seduce her ear. Little sounds escaped her and her body began to writhe.

"How'm I doing?" he breathed it hotly into her ear.

"Quite well. You are, however, neglecting my... thighs."

"Sorry."

"Mmmmm."

After a time, he questioned in a clogged, foggy voice, "Anything I've forgotten?"

"Uh, you haven't, uh, seen if . . . the parts fit yet."

"Oh! Well." He shifted their bodies. "How about . . . thisssss."

"Ahhhh. Ohhhhh, yeesssss."

Some time after that, as they changed the bed linen, she gave him a verbal clearance, showing he was reacting properly to a potential seduction. She said if she could arrange the time that evening, they would have a full, dress rehearsal, just to check him out in case his passing the test had been a fluke.

He was grateful.

She continued, "Anyone can do anything once. We have to be sure performance is at level before any certificate can be issued."

"Of course."

"You might get in a couple of naps, and eat oysters, olives and . . ."

"Of course."

"Is that all you can say?"

"I'm still speechless. In shock. An innocent boy like me tangling with a rapacious woman of the world like you! I have to adjust."

"Good. Be brave."

"That's what all you wicked women say to us innocent young boys."

"Of course."

"That's my line." He kissed her very gently. "Thank God I don't have to go out and do something drastic like mow the yard or drive to the grocery or anything like that.''

She laughed at him.

At noon, when Laura phoned her office, Jeanine said, "Mr. Perry called from Columbia, Laura. Sorry, but it seems his partner's wife wants to do the coordination. She thinks 'It'll be fun.' Sorry, honey. There is some mail, shall I send it on?''

"That'll be fine. Send it to General Delivery, Myrtle Beach, South Carolina.''

"You ought to phone your mother. She called a message in yesterday.''

"Call her for me and tell her I lost the Columbia account and I'll be in touch. Thanks, Jeanine. I'll call tomorrow. Bye.''

When Laura hung up, Tanner inquired, "General Delivery?''

"It's easy to remember. And since you don't get mail here, I thought you had reason not to. Anyway, it's easier for the Post Office to forward it directly if there's anything.''

Tanner explained, "One of the reasons I don't get mail here is that I never stay any place for very long. All I need is the computer and the answering equipment. When I'm through here, I just load the stuff into the car and move to another place and post that number for contacts.''

"A wanderer.''

"My job takes me around.''

She smiled. "Live for today."

"And tonight for my dress rehearsal."

"I believe I'll need a nap."

"Fortunately I have clean sheets on my bed."

"A nap...alone. I can't deplete my resources if I face a dress rehearsal."

"Are you tired, baby?" He smiled and came to her to take her into his arms. "Do I wear you out? You are just too delicious. Let's go sit on the porch and relax, then you can sleep."

Dog sat stolidly on the porch, watching. He turned to look at Tanner and Laura, but he continued his vigil. They cleaned his bowls and freshened the water. She shook the rug and folded it comfortably. And she even leaned down with her hands on her knees to speak to the dog, who watched her gravely.

She straightened and held Tanner's hand as they looked out over their view of the road, the beach and out over the restless Atlantic. The sky was sullen, low, and the breeze humid and fitful. A cold rain was predicted coming across the land, to ruin for a time the promise of summer.

She stretched and smiled up at Tanner and he returned the smile. He led her over to sit on the padded porch swing, and he leaned her against him as he swung it gently. She curled up with her back along his body, and they were contentedly silent.

"Maybe it's a good thing Mr. Perry's plans folded," Laura said. "I haven't done anything for two days."

"I just made love to you last night. Today is the only day I've wasted for you."

"Wasted?" She laughed a lovely, throaty laugh. "For two days I was sewing dresses like mad and planning your seduction."

"That's hardly wasted time."

"I can't hold my eyes open."

He coaxed, "Let's go to bed."

"Oh, no you don't."

He chuckled a rumble in his chest that she could feel in her back. "There's no way I'm going to spoil your seduction of me tonight. Go on upstairs, hussy, and get to your plotting of my downfall." They kissed nicely, and he patted her bottom as she rose from the swing to go upstairs.

The weather forecast said there was an enormous weather system approaching the east coast, there would be rain and the spring storm promised it would become much cooler. With the promised change in weather, she sorted through the guest closet for some long-sleeved sailor blouses made of soft cotton. She also found some trousers of deck cotton with an elastic waist.

In a cavernous, linen storage closet she found another quilt. How carelessly those handmade works of art were actually used on beds when they should have been hung on walls. They were lovely things. She ran her hand over the tiny quilting stitches and appreciated the work involved in making them. She chose an intricate Double Wedding Ring design and carried it to her room. Stripping, she lay down on the bed and pulled the quilt over her, then she snuggled down. Ah, Tanner.

How could this man be so different from other men? She could remember when she was married to Tom and she had wondered "Was that all there was to living?" She'd always had the feeling of being incomplete, of expecting there was more, of missing out.

She and Tom had never had the sharing of humor that she had with Tanner. And the passion! How could it be so different with Tanner? A man was only a man. The parts only fit together. Why was their fitting so different? How could he be the one to make her so aware of him? Why him? How remarkable.

He wanted a relationship. But for how long? He spoke of grandchildren. She lay there somberly thinking of what she wanted and how honest she was in being there with Tanner at this time in his life. He was at a very vulnerable crossroad. Physically weakened, how strong was he emotionally? Could she trust his emotions as being reliable in his own decision concerning his wanting a commitment from her?

They needed to talk.

When she'd heard Pete say Tanner's name again and knew he'd been hurt, her own judgment had gone askew. It was totally foreign for her to have come to him when she had never really known him. And to stay with him so impulsively! With no hesitation at all. That could be instinct.

It could be sex. And now that she knew how miraculous making love with him could be, why this sudden questioning? Why this hesitation? Did she really want to go back into the servitude of marriage? She had only begun to taste the ramifications of independence in these past few years. She'd gone from father to college to husband. She'd never been on her own.

To have divorced Tom had been unusual behavior for her. She had been surprised she had that much courage. But she'd looked down the dull years of sameness and she couldn't stay married to Tom. He'd been offended by the divorce. He'd been bitter and he'd cleaned her out financially.

It had been worth giving up the money and property in order to be free. She'd never felt companionable with Tom. In spite of how hard she tried, they were never friends. It was as if they were cordial acquaintances. She'd never felt fulfilled with Tom. Even when she'd been satisfied, it hadn't been such fulfillment as she'd had the night before with Tanner.

Was her present conduct because she was more mature? Her child-bearing years were waning. Was old mother nature pushing?

She did love him. She cared for and about him. But did she want to risk marriage again? Better just to live with Tanner, keep control of her own life, until this bloom wore off, and he began to treat her the way the men in her experience used women.

She and Tanner had to talk. Yes.

But it wasn't talking with Tanner that made her smile as she drifted into sleep. She slept like a log. Motionless, deep and still. She wakened and smiled before she even remembered Tanner, her love. Ah, Tanner. What was she to do about Tanner?

Seven

When Laura wakened from her nap, she bathed, sprayed her naked body with a faint mist of Chanel No 5 and painted her finger and toenails a bright red. She dressed in lace briefs and that wicked wicked clingy red silk dress with its shadow panel. She put on quite a bit of eye makeup and some red lipstick. She brushed her hair so it fell loosely around her shoulders and she wore those long sparkly, mismatched earrings. Since she had no suitable shoes, she went barefooted.

With the creaky stairs, her descent was heralded, and Tanner was at the bottom of the steps waiting for her. He was in a suit . . . and a bow tie. His unruly hair was parted unsuccessfully in the center and an effort had been made to plaster it down. What a miserable attempt he'd made to look like an innocent rube! She bubbled laughter.

There was no answering laughter. He was solemn and his eyes were glued on her. With him there to witness it, she made a slow-motion production of her descent. "My God," he breathed as he watched her, and she put back her head and laughed. He asked, "That's my dress? The one you made for me?"

"Yes."

He said, "Okay, I give up."

She frowned at him and slumped. "You're really very irritating. Show a little backbone."

"Show backbone? You want me naked? Okay." He reached up to his tie, never taking his eyes from her.

"No! I mean you ought to show a little resistance."

He amended, "I'm not easy, you know."

"I haven't even *asked* you yet!"

He explained, "That dress does it. And I think the bare feet with that outfit are the most erotic thing I've ever seen. It makes you look abandoned."

"Left by the roadside like Dog?"

"No morals." The fires in his blue eyes flamed up as he smiled. He reached for her as she came to the last step and her mouth was almost even with his.

She turned her head as she protested, "You'll smear my lipstick."

So he did. Quite thoroughly. And he made low, throaty sounds while he did that. He looked her over, as she released herself, and he watched her walk as she went to the kitchen. She allowed herself a restrained swish and flirted over her shoulder at him. He leaned against the wall and put one hand to his head to steady himself, making her laugh again.

Her laugh sounded very like that ghost laugh the first night: very knowing. As Tanner followed her into the kitchen, she asked, "Was there a woman here that first night I was here?"

"Why?"

Not "no" but "why?"

"I thought I heard a laugh."

"A nice, sexy laugh?"

She turned around and gave him a startled look. "There *is* a ghost?"

"We aren't sure who she is—or was—but that's all she does. The laugh is such that the men all smile and the women get prickly. You laughed that way last night."

"I don't recall having had any time to laugh."

"The sound's exciting to a man. You laughed that way again, just now, when you came down the stairs, and I knew it wouldn't do me any good at all to resist."

She smiled a slow smile at him, amused.

"Smiles like that drive a man right up the wall." He took a deep breath. "I hope you get to eat your supper."

"This isn't supper, it's dinner." She opened the refrigerator door. The shrimp cocktails were already made up, in two iced bowls with the sauce as a side dish. "You fixed the shrimp and made the sauce!"

"I was restless." He licked his lips.

She gave him a look from under almost closed eye-lashes and whispered in a huskily sexual parody, "Licking lips like that makes a woman lose her mind."

He came to her and smeared what was left of her lipstick. He couldn't be still and he fidgeted like a man who was getting ready to race in competition. He said, "You jiggle."

"It's the dress."

His chuckle was delicious, his hot eyes slid over her, and his hands had to touch her.

She stopped, as he blocked her way and kissed her, holding her to him. She looked up at him and when she could she asked, "Who is seducing whom?"

"I'm not seducing you! I'm just being friendly."

"Very. You're *supposed* to be casual, interested in business, courteous, helpful with the dishes, and completely unsuspecting. You're no challenge at all."

"Unsuspecting? I'm supposed to be unsuspecting with you in that dress? *In that dress?* You must be joshing! I'm surprised I didn't take you on the stairs. It was only my iron restraint—be serious! That kept me from—Laura!"

She handed him the tureen of shrimp creole, and he took a deep, steadying breath. She instructed, "Put it on the table on the pad."

He said, "Hmm?"

She sighed, "You're no challenge at all."

"You want challenge? Madam, and I mean no sly or slanderous innuendo with that address, if you want challenge, you get challenge.'' He carried the tureen into the next room and didn't reappear.

She half waited, then took the shrimp plates from the refrigerator and went into the dining room. He was sitting at his place with his hands neatly folded in front of him. He rose, held her chair and sat back down. He put his napkin on his lap and said, ''The hogs have been doing fine this year. Lots of little hogs and fat, feeding momma hogs. The year is looking good.''

She gave him a patient stare.

''The weeds are growing up between the rows and I'll be all week getting them chopped back.''

In a studied way, she commented, ''I thought bore farming was coming into being. Leaving a covering of old growth on the fields and drilling holes and putting seeds in without plowing.''

''There's no place in a man's world for a smart-tongued woman who reads. Barefoot and pregnant, that's how to keep a woman.''

Something flashed in her eyes.

''This is a right smart meal. How are you at lifting bales and picking cotton?''

''As good as any man.''

He raised his eyebrows and smiled. ''I like you feisty and challenging. How are you at cleaning wells? And the roof needs patching.''

''When I said I needed challenge it was not as a laborer but as a seducer. You aren't supposed to test my muscles, you're supposed to appear unaware of the fact I'm female.''

"With you in *that* dress, I'm supposed to forget you're female?" The idea seemed difficult to him.

Coolly she replied, "Yes."

"Oh. Well." He sipped his wine, as he seemed to reorient himself, then he took a bracing breath, cleared his throat and inquired, "How do you think the Cubs will do this year, old buddy?"

"I'm a Mets fan."

That appeared to rock him back on his mental heels and he asked in a argumentative way, "Now why in the world would you go with the Mets? Their pitching is the pits, they can't catch a ball with a basket and they wobble when they run. Zeros."

She put down her fork.

"Just testing!" He put up both hands from the table. "There are lip-service fans and then there are your kind who wade right in there and slug it out. I don't slug, but I might be tricked into a little wrestling?"

"One never pokes at the loyalty of a Mets fan," she informed him sternly.

"Learn something new every day. Do you drink beer?"

"I've never been able to get past the smell of it."

He nodded.

She elaborated, "I understand the taste is an acquired one."

"Umm. Like olives and raw oysters," he replied. "Do you ski?"

"I like snow skiing, but I'm not really athletic. I'm not skilled enough. Team sports have always been beyond me. I feel I'm hampering the rest, holding them back.''

"I know one sport you do as a partner that is extremely skilled."

"Shhhh!" She was exasperated. "I am working up *gradually*. We aren't supposed to mention anything about it yet."

"Oh."

"What exactly do you do? Why does a car driving by here make you vanish and reappear at the door to see whose it is?"

"The way one stays whole and healthy in this world is to be aware of one's surroundings," he began. "When you said you'd heard a car and then another, I was curious. I called a contact and inquired if there were any hostiles out for scalps. They are checking on it. Since Dog doesn't react to the car, it's not someone searching for him. I asked Milo to—Milo's the area Law—I asked him to keep an eye open."

"There's danger? Someone after you?" She sat straighter feeling quite belligerent and ready to help.

He watched her, thrilled as much by her reaction as by her. Her loyalty included him, right up there with the Mets! "There's no danger. Only cause to be alert. It's probably someone visiting the area. We'll find out."

She asked cautiously, "Someone of those who, you told me, was caught and got mad at the catcher?"

"There's always that possibility."

"What exactly do you do? You said it involved white-collar crimes."

"It's very complicated. My role is less and less physical involvement, especially since the wreck. I'm just not as lively as I was. I mostly check records. I'm a skilled computer hacker. As reported in *Time* magazine's cover report on computers, and in user groups, a hacker is a proud name. A 'cracker' is someone who uses a computer for illegal purposes. They are some of the ones I search out. I watch for 'footprints' showing someone has been snooping in files or records.

"We now have the means to trace the snoopers—the crackers," he continued. "There are all kinds of reasons for people to want to see files. Like watching how someone invests and in which directions, who's selling stocks and bonds, or intruding into more personal files. And we look for unusual bank deposits or withdrawals.

"Most of what I do is part of a greater investigation. There's good reason to suspect something is wrong. I'm small potatoes. What I do is tedious and most investigators haven't the patience for it. I find it fascinating. It's a chess game of sleuthing. The criminal is clever and I have to be more so.

"I'm not the only one doing this. There's a network of us. We compare notes and make suggestions. We work to keep confidential files confidential. We try to keep ahead of the criminal element. White-collar criminals are just as wicked as the ordinary crooks. Anyone who cheats someone else has a flaw that could jeopardize our country if the price was right. There's no villain greater than that." He shifted in his chair and smiled at her. "Sorry. I get carried away."

Quite seriously she said, "I'm proud of your feelings for our country."

"I don't like cheaters. It isn't just the biggies. It's also the guy who thinks the laws are for everyone *else*, who runs stop signs, and ignores speed limits, and gets mad at the cop who catches him. Then he's surprised when his kid cheats."

"How did you get into this particular field?"

He opened out his hands as if to reveal it all. "After Nam I was at odds with the world. It was a stupid war. We had no business there. It was so unorganized. There was us against everything else, armies that weren't armies, fighting that was completely different—no lines drawn, no identifying uniforms, chaos. It was a strange experience and one to age you fast, if you survived it.

"It seemed to me the easiest thing to do, in order to solve the problems of mankind, was to reorganize the world into a more identifiable system. Separate things out better. And computers came along, the personal ones anyone could have, that lead the way to another form of almost instant communication. It was astonishing. The scope of computer communication and storage, the potential, is just boggling. It's like our brains. We still don't know how our brains really work or how to use the rest of them. And computers are like that.

"I was a pioneer hacker when the modem came along." He paused and explained, "A modem allows computer-to-computer communication via telephone. And there were other people who were fascinated. Hackers learned the ramifications possible with the modem. Learning the usage takes time. So a lot of my first contacts were kids fifteen and sixteen who had the time to explore the scope of computer communication. They're all older now. Some have drifted into other fields, but there are still a core of us who are very involved in the detection of devious intrusions."

By then they were spooning sherbet from frosted bowls. And their wine bottle had been replaced. They sat back and smiled at each other and Tanner said, "So what makes Laura tick?"

"You do."

"My God, what an opening line," he said quietly.

"I'm glad I know you."

"I return that wondrous thought."

"The wind has picked up and it's getting quite cool. Don't you think Dog should come inside?"

"Is that Laura Fullerton, disgusted dog dodger, actually inviting a canine into her castle?"

"It's just a little chilly out and he's been very weather worn."

"I'll ask if he'd like to join us."

Dog hesitated. He went out to the steps and looked down along the road, then he came back to the door and looked up at Tanner. But he didn't come inside.

He'd indicated he understood the invitation, but that he must keep the vigil.

Tanner went to the storage room and found a sturdy cardboard box, one that had held some of the swatches he'd ordered for Laura. He took the box out on the porch and set it down so Dog could go inside it out of the wind and still see the road.

Laura watched Tanner do all that. His actions touched her heart.

"It's really cold," he said. "I need to go around and close a few windows. And then I'll build us a fire in the library. We can take our wine in there."

While Tanner closed windows and brought in wood, Laura filled the dishwasher. When that was done, she went into the library with a feeling of inevitability.

He'd brought in the pad from the swing, for it was beginning to spit rain, and he laid it on the floor in front of the fire. He brought a plush throw from a closet and laid it on top of the pad, then he collected pillows from around the lower floor. They now had a Sultan's nest.

He took off his jacket, pulled the bow tie loose, then undid the top several buttons of his shirt and rolled up the sleeves. He slid off his shoes and dropped down into the nest as he said, "Bring on the dancing girls." Then he poured more wine in their glasses.

"We need some music."

"I could hum," he offered.

"Some lovely, soft music. No record player?"

"You're being very picky." He got up and went outside to his car, got some tapes, stopped off in his room for a tape player and returned to the fire and Laura.

He put in a tape and set the tape player to one side. Then he sank down beside Laura and kissed her. His hair was tousled and wet and his shoulders were damp from his trip outside to his car. "Anything else? Tell me now."

"I can't of think anything that's out of reach." She grinned.

"Oh yes?"

"Oh, yes." And she kissed him.

"Ahhhh. At last."

She piled up pillows and curled on her side, then she directed him so that he lay with his head on her thighs. She asked him, "Who was your first love?"

"You."

"How quick you are. A diplomat."

"I didn't know what love was until I knew you at school. You used to make my nights into the most sensual, the most frustrating madness. It was tougher than the war. Then I was only terrified, but with you I had no hope."

"Why didn't you ever ask me out?"

"You were going with Mike. And when I heard you'd broken up with him, you were already engaged to Tom. You never gave any indication that you noticed me."

"I noticed you."

"Kiss me."

She scolded, "I'm in control here. I'll let you know when there's kissing to be done."

"Now?"

"Yes."

"You drive me mad."

"I don't know exactly what you do to me, but it scares me. I'm glad you're free. You aren't involved with any woman, are you?"

"You."

"Oh, Tanner..." She curled around so that his head was on some pillows and she was across his chest as she kissed him. She raised her mouth to breathe, and he nudged it down, holding the back of her neck, controlling her. In a foggy voice she asked, "I'm not hurting you, am I?"

"You're killing me," he told her gruffly. But as she tried to lift from his chest, he held her there. "You're paralyzing me." And he showed her how.

"All of you is so tense. How different we are. I'm like mush, and you're like rock."

He smoothed his hands on the dress down her, his palms taking sensual pleasure from the feel of the silklike material on her feminine body. "You made the dress for me?"

"To attract you."

"It's like silk on satin." His hands confirmed that. "I think it's interesting you felt I wasn't paying you any attention."

"I'm glad the dress pleases you, the stuff is ghastly to sew. It slithers."

"Take off my shirt and slither on me."

"You make me sound like a snake."

"Wind around me."

She chuckled low in her throat and his eyes burned into her. His breath was a steam blast, and his hands scorched her. He commanded, "Touch me."

She smoothed his hair back from his face. "Your hair is very independent." Her fingers slowly combed through the rough silk, but he twitched with impatience. She leaned and kissed him, but he took over and turned the sweet meeting of their lips into a devouring feeding of a starving man. She pushed a space between their mouths and said, "You're rushing." By then she was on her back, and he loomed above her. He kissed her again—his way—and she laughed.

"What's funny?" he growled.

"This here 'rube' is betraying himself. You lied. You're no innocent country boy."

"Oh, I forgot I'd used that old tack," he rumbled in her ear as he did all sorts of sensational things to it with his tongue and nibbling lips and breath. "Undo my shirt."

"Do I look like a valet?"

"I'd interview you for the job."

"Let's see, I suppose we undo the buttons first? Or does it come off over your head?"

"Try the buttons," he suggested.

"They are lapped over wrong. What a silly way to button a shirt. Backward."

"I'm used to it. You're doing very well. You can have the job."

"The belt buckle's wrong too. We'll have to change that."

"I could just not wear any clothes at all." He was helpful.

"Great! But then how would I justify being your valet?"

"We could think of something for you to do."

"I don't do windows...."

He kissed her, gently rubbing his chest against her silky softness and he purred in his throat with the sensual sensation. "Oh, Laura..." His breath seemed to steam, and his hot hands were hard on her silken curves.

She'd already lost one earring and her hair was tumbled in a very careless and attractive way. Her eyes felt heavy and her lips pouted as if waiting for his. She was quite languid in her movements while he was almost feverish in his. When he manipulated her to suit himself, it felt as if she was boneless.

As she stretched, she moved slowly, and he began to tremble. He pushed the straps from her shoulders and smoothed the material from her breasts so he could look at her there in the firelight. "Ah, Laura, you are so beautiful."

"Tanner..."

They spoke in incomplete sentences, with the need to talk to each other, to hear their voices, but with nothing to say. As they moved in their dance of love, tempting completion, there were moans and gasps and turnings as they followed the patterns of enticement. Their thighs rubbing, their hands seeking, their lips caressing. Their faces stroking along the other in their passion, as they made love.

Her dress and briefs were abandoned into a small fiery heap and his clothes were discarded. They lay naked in the firelight as they entwined, their need accelerating, their movements hungrier, their hands rougher, fingers tensed and pressing. She was frantic and on fire. The storm's sound rising outside the house played the counterpoint of their crescendo, heightening their emotion with the elemental sound.

Tanner orchestrated their love with great finesse and carried her on that exquisitely thrilling experience to its ultimate release, and to the spiraling aftermath with its delicious echoes of passion.

Still awed by the scope of their love making, they lay coupled, depleted. He moved to put his arms under her, bracing himself painfully on healing muscles as he held her, cherished her and hugged her to him. Then he moved from her carefully, in spite of her small sounds of protest, and he lay on his back beside her, trembling now with the residue of his expenditure of power.

With only a minute of rest, he rolled up onto his elbow to lean over her, watching her, his breath still not steadied, and he kissed her, his sweat dripping, his hand still shaking with his spent passion. "Laura..."

She smiled softly, sleepily. "You are simply fabulous."

"So are you. Beautiful."

"Let's do it again." She was boneless and droll.

"Okay. Any time next week."

"Next *week*?"

"I might be somewhat recovered by then."

Lazily she chuckled. "I never had a chance."

"True. You're mine. What chance?"

Her voice slow, she explained, "My great seduction! All that work making the dress and compiling the perfect meal, and you never gave me any chance at all!"

"You'll have the next time. You'll have full control. I won't move a muscle. I'll hum and look out the window." He kissed her very gently on her eyes and cheeks and chin. Her lips were available, and she turned her face to help him, but he ignored them and went on with her forehead and temples, her nose.

"I can use all my wiles the next time?"

"I promise."

She raised up, and he allowed that, and she pushed so that he went on over to lie on his back. She smiled and her eyes danced.

He demurred, "Laura."

"Be still."

"Sweetheart, there's possibility and then probability, but there's 'not now,' too. Honey, uh, careful.

Why don't you just lie back and rest a while? Uh. I'm a little tender there.''

"It was only just a few minutes ago that you *put* my hand there. Why then and not now?'' she inquired with a great, contrived, need to know.

"How about a nice little nap?''

"Your attention span leaves something to be desired.'' She shook her head, then she did it again so her hair tickled his chest.

"We'll get back to the desire part in a week or maybe two. You're a tiger. I believe you're the woman they were warning us about in basic training. They said there were women like you who use up nice boys for their own pleasure. We were warned to beware.''

"Kiss me.''

"I might manage a handshake.''

She lay back with a delicious laugh and they held hands.

He murmured, "I never dreamed I would ever be so lucky to find you again and love you. This is a dream.''

"Isn't it.''

"Did I satisfy you? Was it good for you?''

"Oh, Tanner. You are fantastic. I had never known what love was like. I was married for almost two years, but I never had such love. You are perfect.''

And their conversation went on that way as they debated who was the greater lover. They never agreed. They lay in the firelight, still naked, touching, petting, smiling, teasing, laughing, murmuring. And they made love again some long time after that. Gentle love. Not frantic or wild but sweet tender love. And as the fire crumbled into only feeble coals they slept.

The beep wakened Tanner like a bolt of lightning. He was up and into the study in the wink of an eye. Laura felt him leave, and his urgency alarmed her. She waited, hearing a whirl and two computer sounds. Then silence.

She got up, picked up her dress and slipped it on before she went cautiously into the hall. All was dark. There was a glow in the study and she walked carefully to that door.

Tanner was naked in the subtle light, and she was aware how beautifully made he was even as she questioned, "What is it?"

He was taking several pieces from inside his computer. There was a basket and in it he'd put the tracer, the filter, the scrambler and several other parts from his computer. He didn't even look up but said tersely, "We're leaving. Grab a change of clothes and any important papers. We'll probably be very isolated. Take what you'll need. We'll leave anything else. Take only what can *not* be replaced."

"What are you doing?"

"These are enhanced cards, expanded, I'm taking with us. Hurry!"

"Tanner..."

"I'll explain everything later. Hurry!"

Eight

It was still blowing and raining outside and quite cool. What time was it? Laura wondered. It was long after midnight. In her room Laura pulled off the seduction dress and put on a worn cotton jump suit from the guest closet. She looked around, mentally sorting as she discarded her possessions. She grabbed several pairs of underwear and her toothbrush to stuff them in her purse.

What did she actually need? She took the thongs, then a pair of her pumps that had low heels. She folded the two cotton sailor middies and the pair of elastic-topped trousers she'd found earlier in the guest closet and set aside to wear in the cooler weather. And she took a large bandanna to carry it all in, like a hobo's pack.

She snatched her lined raincoat, which any traveler carries in the spring and fall, and took her purse. She left her two suits and their blouses neatly hanging in the closet with her high-heeled pumps lined up underneath.

Rushing down to the morning room, she took a deep breath for courage in order to ignore the treasures she would have to leave behind. She scooped up her folder, some pencils, the crayons, and eyed the butcher paper with regret, before she caught up her sketch pad. She gave a last, quick, regretful glance around at the tumble of materials in a cascade of colors before she hurried to the study.

Tanner wasn't there. She went back toward his room, but at the kitchen she found him putting some fruit into a plastic bag. He was dressed much as she was, and he had the handled wicker basket, which held his computer parts, by him on the floor. Tense, he gave her a quick smile as he laid the fruit on top of the computer parts and reached for her folded clothes. He carelessly disordered the clothing as he put them on top of the basket. It looked like a laundry basket.

"Why are we doing this?" A very logical question.

"The cars that have been going by aren't local," he explained. "We're still not sure my wreck was an accident. We're just being careful."

"Someone could be . . . after you?"

"We're just being sure."

"Oh." Then she asked in quick concern, "What about Dog?"

"I'll call Henry in the morning and ask him to take the dog back. Dog has enough food and water. And his rug in that box will keep him warm." But when they went out to the car, Dog was there to watch them inquiringly. And when Tanner opened the car door, Dog got in.

"He knows we're leaving." Laura looked at the calm dog then to Tanner.

"Dogs are smart," he agreed. "Let's go."

"Where?"

"There are always contingency plans. We're directed to use our plan B."

"Is this really serious?" Laura was still having trouble with their exodus.

"Probably not."

"Oh. *Probably* not. That's why we're sneaking out after—" she looked at her watch "—three in the morning, going God only knows where?"

"I have to make some quick contacts on the CB. It will be in code. I can't miss any segments. So you must not talk. I'll tell you all about it later."

Apparently Tanner's contact did communicate sensible information, in the brief combinations of letters and numbers with station switches, for they hadn't gone twenty miles when Tanner pulled up, flicked his lights and a Chevy came up in back of them.

In a terse voice Tanner told her, "Wait here until I'm sure." He got out cautiously and stood by his door, and so did a man from the Chevy. Again they spoke in letters and numbers. Then Tanner leaned down and said to Laura, "It's okay. Let's go."

The whole episode was so unreal that it bordered very closely on ridiculous and Laura felt the semihysterical nudging impulse to giggle. She got out of the Porsche, into the rain, Dog followed unquestioningly, and they walked to the Chevy. The other man held her door, and Dog hopped into the back without being told.

Tanner told the man, "Take care of the Porsche."

"With pleasure," the man replied. Then he added, "Good luck."

Tanner lifted a hand, got into the Chevy, backed away from the Porsche, and they took off down the road.

Laura looked back through the rain-splattered rear window and saw the Porsche's lights sweep around as it headed back through the rain toward Myrtle Beach. She turned forward again to sit and stare out the windshield, which was relentlessly swept by the wipers, and her eyes were big and her adrenaline pretty high.

She turned her head to check on the dog, but he'd curled up on the back seat. He opened his steady eyes and watched her. She faced forward again, scrunched down in her coat and was silent.

The car hurried through the dark and rainy night, and Tanner's profile was serious but calm. He was a good man to have around. He was a good man period. He was important to her. What in the world was going on? Well, obviously it had to be some white-collar crook who bore a grudge.

If Tanner was in danger then she was, too. She looked out into the stormy night. It was strange, she didn't feel scared. Not yet. She felt…like manning the battlements. Womaning them. That was an odd reaction. She was a card-carrying coward. Why this defensive reaction for danger to Tanner? She loved him. She did understand that. But he was a whole lot better trained to deal with danger than she was. Why should she feel so strong and combative in his protection?

She thought back over their short week together, reviewing his actions with finding and caring for the dog, and his gentleness with her. She also thought of their conversations. And she knew she thought he was valuable, not only to her, but to the country as a whole.

Tanner was a doer. She was on his side. She leaned back. She was his partner in whatever came. She would see to it he survived. Then her mind was entertained with scenes of her protecting Tanner, and she had to smile it was all so silly.

This wasn't silly. For a man like Tanner to leave for parts unknown in the middle of the night was deadly serious. A little shiver went up her spine. She must obey him exactly. These people knew what they were doing. She could ruin any of their plans by being stupid. She would be very careful.

After a time there were more cryptic communications via the citizens band radio. And Tanner gave minimal reponses.

Laura listened silently, asking none of the myriad questions, nor did she offer any of the avalanche of comments. Those did pile up. Why those symbols? Did they change? How did he remember them? Who thought up the codes that Tanner and the unseen voices were using? Little old ladies in apartments with geraniums in the pots and cats by the fire? How would they dispense the information? Did they mail out a weekly newsletter?

Codes too were probably done by computer. All the romance was gone from spying. Not wit against wit, but computer against computer. Of course someone had to run the computer and tell it what to do and to understand what was needed to make it do exactly that.

Computers took some of the magic from human endeavor. But that magic was replaced by opening up such computer resources! It wasn't like physics, which took the magic away by explaining everything and making it ordinary and understandable. The scope of computer potential was limitless. Just with color schemes! With a computer an artist could view sixteen hundred combinations of color in eye blinks of time.

Five lifetimes weren't enough to experience all the wonders of living. That was one reason she believed in reincarnation. God could never be so unkind as to give us each just a taste of the wonders of living and then let it end. Laura's mind twirled on, entertaining herself, as she dozed. And before dawn they arrived...somewhere.

The weather was clearer inland. The clouds moved with the wind and there was occasional moonlight. In it, they saw the house that was small and isolated. It was tucked into a dimple of earth and surrounded by acres of trees. Even a searching eye would have a hard time finding it. They wouldn't have found it if they hadn't had exact directions. It was a hideaway.

The Chevy moved down the faint track through the trees. The house was unpainted and blended well. The garage doors were open. Tanner drove the Chevy into the gloom of that haven and turned off the motor. They sat in the silence.

Softly Laura said the obvious, "We're here."

He touched her arm. "I'm glad you're with me but I wish you weren't."

They got out of the car and stretched, and Dog also stepped down from the car and looked around before he nosed out the door and walked around with curiosity.

Tanner took the basket from the car's trunk, and as he closed the garage doors on squeakless hinges the back door of the house opened and a tall man stood there. He queried, "K?"

And Tanner replied in a jumble of letters and numbers. It was all strange to Laura.

"Welcome." The man was long-limbed like Tanner and he came outside in an easy slouch, his hands in his pockets. "So you brought her along." His eyes stabbed at Laura.

Laura looked at Tanner who said, "There was no way I could leave her. She's okay."

"No one is."

"As I'm okay, so is she."

"Ah," he said in response. "I'm Brodwick."

Tanner shook hands. "I've heard a thing or two about you. This is Laura Fullerton. Honey, this is Brodwick."

Brodwick gave a formal nod to Laura but he replied to Tanner, "I've heard a thing or two about you, Tanner. We have a computer set up in the living room. Use it, do as you please. There's an override for messages. You must be a genius! We have orders to take very good care of you. You're valuable, but, as I understand it, a lousy driver." Brodwick smiled ruefully as he referred to the wreck.

Responding to the easy ribbing, Tanner explained, "Well, there was a ditch with trees. Solid, big trees with awesome root systems that keep them upright."

"That would influence an evasive action. You look mobile."

"Getting there."

"Let me carry that?" They moved into the softly lighted house. "You brought the scrambler?"

"And my cards."

"Good. I'll enjoy seeing them. I heard you're innovative."

"I'd be pleased. You have any here?"

"None here." Brodwick shook his head. "We had to get you some place fast and this was closest."

"Something going?"

"We didn't chance it. Better safe than sorry, to coin a phrase. You kids hungry?" He called them kids but he wasn't much older.

Tanner asked, "Do you have anything for the dog? He was abandoned or lost and he's had a couple of days on regular chow and has probably gotten used to eating."

"When I saw the dog I understood you bringing him. He's a dandy. Is that a new flea collar?"

"Yes."

"Is he trained at all?"

"I've never been around a trained animal. He's obedient. But if he's a pro or not—" Tanner shrugged his shoulders "—I have no idea. He's loyal. It was his idea to come along."

"I'll check him out after I feed him. If he allows me to feed him on command that will tell us something. Come along and I'll show you the 'dungeon.'"

He led the way into the kitchen and through a door, down stairs to the basement. He slid aside a false wall, pushed a light switch sideways, touched a concealed button, and a section of brick moved.

They entered, Laura unbelieving of anything so bizarre, and they were shown how to close both the false wall and shut the section of brick. Flashlights were stacked on a shelf, and the tunnel went off out of sight, lighted minimally with something like Christmas wheat lights at spaced intervals. It was sufficient light. Laura simply stared.

In a perfectly normal voice, as if their circumstances were not unusual, Brodwick explained to Tanner so that Laura too could hear and understand, "If push came to shove, if someone came into the tunnel without the password, or if the place was on fire, you'd go on down the tunnel. It exits along the creek into bushes. Be very careful under those circumstances. Unless you must, don't leave the tunnel for two days. Someone would come if we didn't report in.

"We've never *yet* had to use the tunnel," he said bracingly as Tanner went through the procedure. "It's only precautionary. We don't even know if there's a problem for you. We were all Boy Scouts and take the motto Be Prepared quite seriously. It's only fair you're prepared too. Now, Laura, you work the walls in reverse."

She did, and she watched the light-switch plate slide automatically back into place. It was all unreal. After that they went back up the basement stairs.

"You two can have the second bedroom," Brodwick told them. "The bath works adequately. Food in the fridge. Make yourselves at home. I'll be out and around. Two others are assigned here. They'll be in about noon. We should know what's up shortly or if anything is happening. We're still going over the cases you've worked on, and as you know, it all takes time. But it shouldn't be long before we have a handle on this thing. We're watching your house on the coast. Relax. Enjoy." And with a half wave, he left them.

Tanner turned to Laura. "Okay?"

"This is weird."

"Granted."

"Have you ever done anything like this before?"

"No. That's why we're doing it this time. I can take care of me. I'm expendable. You're not. I won't risk anything happening to you. When they told me the car that kept going by the beach house was driven by a stranger, I would have waited it out, but with you there, I opted for running."

"Oh, Tanner." She went to him. He took her into his arms and held her almost too hard. Her fingers spread out to touch as much of him as her hands could reach. Danger to herself wasn't as important to Laura as danger to Tanner. Her hands went from his head to his shoulders, smoothing, feeling the reality of him. Nothing must happen to Tanner.

He kissed her temple and eased away from her. "You have to be hungry, let's eat."

"Somehow I'm not." She rubbed her face. "But I would like to stretch out."

"Come, let's see what's in the kitchen."

The little house was furnished with only the essentials. The furniture was as anonymous as the facade of the house. No rugs; shades but no curtains. No bedspreads, although the four twin beds were neatly made and blankets folded at the foot of each bed.

In the kitchen there was ample food, paper plates and cups, plastic spoons. It was clean and tidy. Without interest, they poked through the cupboards and refrigerator and mentioned what they found. Each was trying to coax the other to eat something.

There were doughnuts, sugared and squishy, and they each absently ate one and drank a small paper cup of milk.

After they finished, they stuffed their cups into the plastic waste sack. They went to the bedroom Brodwick had indicated they were to use and closed the door. With a very serious expression, Tanner watched Laura as he helped her undress. He lifted the sheet for her to crawl into bed, then he shook out a blanket and covered her.

He stood there watching her eyes following his movements as he slowly took off his own clothes, crowded into the small bed and into her welcoming arms. And he made love to her. He said nothing, and in the silence of that different kind of loving, she too was silent. Their loving was as strange as their circumstances. Dictated by their danger. It was no lighthearted coupling. It was another of the many echelons of love.

Her skin prickled in response. The threat of danger had stiffened her body. Her body still was tense, and now it was hungry. The tips of her fingers dug into his shoulders, and her knees and hips urged him.

Their coupling took on a kind of desperation. His taking her wasn't from body need as much as it was a declaration of possession. She was his. All of him possessed her. His mouth searched her with a deliberation as if his hot kisses branded her as his. And his hands searched her out, his fingers strong and demanding. His body was sure and powerful. And when he finally took them to a shuddering completion, Laura fiercely held him to her as he slid into a deep sleep. For she too was possessive. Tanner was hers.

The three men came separately into the house for lunch so only one was inside at a time. The other two prowled the grounds. It was an apt term for their actions. They were like civilized beasts. The way they walked, moved and the way their eyes watched. They were soft-spoken, they assessed Tanner and Laura before they saw the two "visitors" as personalities.

Besides Brodwick, there were Daniels and Reed—all long-limbed, easygoing men. Tanner was very like them. Tall, well-made. Quiet. No hearty jokes or backslapping. They were from the same breed.

It was Reed who told them, "We put two operators into your beach house. They drove the Porsche in just like home folks. They found a bug on your car. Good thing you switched cars."

Tanner's head snapped up. "They did? I thought I was careful. Was it a new bug?"

"We don't know. You did travel a ways, and they could have used one that had been used before. As to not finding it, it could have been put there at the last minute." Reed shrugged.

"A...bug?" Laura's eyes widened in amazement. Such things only happened in books and films.

But it was Tanner who supplied the reply. "For a tracer. It's a good thing we changed cars."

Neither man appeared alarmed. Reed looked over at Laura. "We couldn't find an agent that fast with your hair color, so she has on a wig."

"Could it be dangerous for them?" Laura asked.

"They are very, very good." Reed smiled at her, his eyes lazy. Then he said to Tanner, "Since you chose to use the crutch when Laura first arrived, he's using a cane." There was an amused, almost unnoticeable stretching out of the words.

Laura realized then that someone had to have been watching over them all along! How else would they know about her or of the fact that Tanner had used a crutch to fool her? Had they watched at the Moran house? Or was it in Myrtle Beach? When? It was spooky to realize anyone could be watched and not have a clue it was happening. It didn't make her feel protected, but a little hostile.

"That dog is really something," Reed commented. "Had him long?"

"He was either abandoned or lost," Tanner replied. "He'd apparently been on the beach for several days. He kept watching the road."

"He isn't a security dog, but he's very intelligent. We've already taught him to bark when we clear our throats. And we're teaching him hand signals. He's eager, or else bored because he's so unchallenged, and glad to be occupied. He looks back along your trail. Wish he could talk."

"I was careful." Tanner said. "Especially with Laura there."

"You have good reason. Don't fret. This is our job, and we're like Dog. We hate being idle."

Apparently Daniels was in charge, it was he who gave them permission to be outside. "Never be out of sight of the house, but only in a circle around it. There's a nice little creek and just below us a fishing hole. You can fish." He smiled. "Or if you're talented enough, you can skip stones. Wear the jump suits and the hats. No use advertising our presence here."

The jump suits were in mottled greens and browns. Camouflage. That was what really brought home to Laura the reality of what was happening. They had to hide. Someone could be hunting them...to do them harm.

When she got back home again to South Bend, Indiana, Laura decided she was going to take judo and karate. Maybe even get marksman expertise, if she could learn to be comfortable with guns. She muddled over the facts of life, the ramifications of living in this dangerous world.

Tanner's strong hand covered hers. "You'll be all right." His voice was calm, but tension lived in his body unabated.

She wasn't the only one who saw how tightly triggered Tanner was. He never relaxed. It seemed each man, Brodwick, Daniels and Reed all sought to make things seem ordinary and to make this impossibly abnormal situation appear placid and unthreatening. Even as they checked their guns, and moved soundlessly away to watch, they talked of mundane things. "Weather's beautiful for this time of year. Different where I come from," Reed offered.

"Where'd you come from?" Laura felt invited to ask.

"Up north of here." He smiled in apology for the close-out reply.

Brodwick told them, "We're going to have a contest as to who catches the biggest fish from that hole in the creek. I want high stakes because I'll win."

"You any good as a cook?" Daniels asked Tanner. He ignored Laura as a candidate.

"I do fairly well," Laura offered.

But Daniels protested, "You're a guest! You mustn't work. We'd be embarrassed to ask a guest to pitch in."

"I believe that's a psychological trick to get me to volunteer," she guessed. He seemed very shocked and so elaborately offended that she laughed.

Whoever was off duty would lure Tanner into explaining how he'd altered his cards for his computer.

To Laura, it was as if they spoke another language. The words were English, but they made no sense at all.

As the afternoon waned and evening came along, Tanner and Laura put on their camouflage jump suits and the floppy camouflage hats, and they went out into the soft light to be joined by Dog.

They walked only as far as directed. But they were outside when the helicopter was first heard. It was Daniels who jerked them under the shield of some trees.

"What...?"

"Not a word." Daniels squatted with them. But the helicopter flew straight across with no side trips or circling.

An insignificant-looking band on Daniels's wrist said, "One of ours."

Daniels lifted the same wrist and replied, "X."

That night as the lovers lay in the single bed, crowded close, Laura said, "This all seems pretty strange and unreal."

Tanner held her tightly to him and didn't reply. His arms hugged her almost too tightly. And his love making was again very strongly possessive. It was as if he could never get enough of her. He didn't allow her night clothes. "I'll keep you warm." And his hands on her were feverish, greedy.

He drove her mad with desire. She tried to smother the sounds of passion that escaped her, and she was embarrassed by the rustle of the bed clothes and the furtive movements of the bed. She was on fire, and his mouth scalded her. She shivered with the heat of him and almost fought for him to take her. He delayed as if he needed her frantic.

His hands were so hot, rubbing down her body, and his heat burned her as she was pressed against him. His desire for her raged in him, but he was silent as he made this strange kind of love to her. His hands shaking. His breath rasping, laboring as he worked at her, undistracted, intense, shivering with his need.

It wasn't "making love" but something else entirely. Were they using their coupling to prove they lived? That they were whole and together? It was as strange as the rest of the adventure. As puzzling.

Not really understanding, Laura did as he wanted, wanting him, wanting to fulfill whatever it was he needed from her. With skill he prolonged the exquisite agony in keeping her on edge for an endless time before finally taking her to completion, exhausting himself and her. And at last they slept.

Nine

———

The next morning, Daniels told them, "There's nothing going on at the coast. Zero. No cars. Not even a stray jogger."

"False alarm." Tanner said it as if he was casual.

"We'll make sure."

"I appreciate the fact you take this seriously."

"There was the bug on your car. When it was put there or for what specific purpose, we don't know, but it was there... and we left it in place for now, out of curiosity. They've been driving the Porsche around looking for a tail. It gives them something to do."

The days passed. Nothing happened. Laura reported in to her office, she worked on current projects. They gave her more paper and pencils. They already had a pencil sharpener.

Laura volunteered to fix supper one night. She made a meat loaf using some of the boggling supply of hamburger. And she made a pie using pudding mix for the filling. They were nice about the meal, but they went back to fried hamburgers with ice cream for dessert.

She did endless sketches of Tanner as he worked on the computer or talked with the other men. She sketched them, too, but they secretly, regretfully burned her drawings. They could allow no pictures. She did drawings of the dog and gradually became friends with him. He was learning more commands and was very clever. They all enjoyed his company.

Accompanied by Dog, the guests walked often through the picture postcard setting. They went through the piney woods with its young underbrush and the cushioning carpet of needles. In the spots the sun found, there were tiny flowers, and in the deep shade there were toadstools and mushrooms. It could have been idyllic, but Tanner never really relaxed.

The pond was lovely. There were trees that reached out their limbs overhead, and the new leaves cast shadows on the surface of the greeny gray pond. They fished and watched the dimpling of the pond as the watery residents chose surface bugs instead of the tempting, baited hooks.

They were never far from a shelter under which they could duck on command. The three guardians never relaxed their vigilance.

When some mushroom hunters went through a corner of the woods, Tanner and Laura were sent to the tunnel for a tense time. The mushroom hunters didn't come near the house, apparently didn't know it was there or that they were avidly watched. After a time the intruders went off.

Of course their car's license number was traced. The car belonged to a high school physics teacher whose wife worked as a check-out clerk at a grocery. Their companions were another teacher and his friend. They had no connection with anyone Tanner had ever known or investigated. It was a false alarm.

There were other false alarms. A plane flying low and circling turned out to be hunting a stray horse. A car that cruised and parked in the woods was an amorous couple who ducked a suspicious husband.

But it was an all-day Boy Scout camp-out that gave them the fidgets. Boys tend to roam and are so intensely curious. And they tell about things, like a tunnel that emerges in bushes by a creek. But even that threat to their solitude passed harmlessly.

Tanner was busy, using the now exquisitely enhanced computer to help research his past cases for some clue to explain their present circumstances, living in a hideaway under protection. So he worked hard. Tanner could work wherever there was a computer.

Then there was Laura who had a business that she was neglecting. She needed to complete her projects, search for other prospects and reschedule postponed appointments. Something had to be decided.

As April drew to a close, there were decisions that would have to be made. The decoy couple in the Moran house on the coast would soon be inundated with Morans, who quite understandably would be intensely curious as to why a strange couple was living there. They would have to leave. There was Tanner's Porsche. Should it be left where it was? Sold? Stored?

Daniels said, "We could move you to an apartment in St. Louis. We could change your identity, go the whole course. Or you could stay here forever, but that might be a drag. We three are darling, but you might occasionally like to see other faces, buy your own supplies, that kind of fun thing. Talk about it."

In their room Laura said to Tanner, "I'll do whatever you decide."

And he replied, "I love you. Never forget that I do. But we need to split. You need to be free of me. We have no idea who's doing this or what's going on, or even if anything is! Laura, I can't stand to have you in any danger. I have decided to give you up."

He sat on the side of their bed but he wouldn't look at her. She reached out to him, but in a strangely harsh voice he said, "For God's sake, don't touch me."

She was stunned. "Tanner..."

"Don't say anything. It must be this way. If anything happened to you, Laura, I don't know what I'd do."

"We could go away. We could find a place to live. You are enough for me."

"If anyone is really looking for me, they'll find me. Wherever we were, I could never quit worrying about you. I can't live that way."

"There is risk to everything we do in our lives, Tanner. In any decision. I could live with risk. I will."

"No." He shook his head. "Don't you realize what that would do to me? I can't see you in jeopardy." With a groan he turned and took her into his arms and made that desperate love with her. As if there would never be another time.

When they lay spent, she said very low and seriously. "But to live without you would be another kind of death. I can't handle that."

"Oh, Laura..." And a ragged, choked breath escaped his iron control.

Laura could guess some of what haunted Tanner. But could she solve it? Carefully she acted as ordinarily as the situation could allow. She thought of things that were amusing, their guardians helped with that, and she talked to Tanner as if their circumstances weren't so strange.

Her efforts were wasted. Despite his facade of languor, his muscles were never uncoiled. He was constantly ready for danger. He was exhausting himself.

To live as they were was so unreal. There in that lovely April weather, with wild flowers growing in charming clumps, with the weather smiling down, or raining down, in the ideal setting of a cabin in the woods and discreetly kind caretakers. It was very strange to live as hostage to an unknown.

Their nemesis finally appeared one beautiful day. They'd been fishing and were going back to the house with their catch, when a man holding a gun stepped from behind a tree like an apparition. He was simply there. So quietly, so amazingly still. They couldn't believe their eyes. But Dog growled.

That drew Laura's eyes to the dog. He had never growled. Why now? And she looked again at the life-threatening stranger who confronted them.

"Just me," Tanner's voice was a soft command. He almost smiled in a terrifyingly wolfish way. Here was his adversary, and he was known to Tanner. "Leave her out of it." Tanner appeared to drift from Laura's side without actually moving. And Dog moved the other way, silent now.

The man said, "Yeah."

"You're Rockwell. Does your uncle know you're here? Tell me that."

"I'm here on my own. I'm going to take you out. I've been in prison all this time because of you."

"You don't learn easily, do you? You went to jail because you manipulated those securities. I only caught you at it.'' Tanner had moved farther from Laura.

Rockwell's voice was a dog's snarl. "If it hadn't been for you, I'd have made it. No one else had a clue."

"How did you find me?" Tanner's voice was almost conversational.

"I hired some private investigators, just like anyone else." He turned his head and looked then at Laura, and his eyes narrowed.

In that split second, Tanner moved. He was a blur of camouflage against the wind-tossed background. At the same moment, snarling viciously, Dog attacked.

Dog's attack was probably what caused Rockwell's first shot to miss. As Tanner hit the man, knocking him over, there was another shot, which plowed along the ground. And after that, there was a wild, dog-growling, man-grunting melee as two of the guardians ran up from opposite directions.

Daniels ordered the dog aside and pulled Tanner from Rockwell. Tanner's avid eyes immediately sought Laura, who was standing there in wide-eyed shock. He went to her and grasped her arms to shake her just a little to be sure she was alive. She said, "Oh, Tanner!" in shuddering disbelief. He put his arms around her and hugged her too tightly as he groaned with his relief... or was it a growl of triumph?

For the moment no one paid any attention to the body still on the ground. Rockwell didn't get up. His neck was broken.

The two guards hurried Tanner and Laura to the house and ordered them to the basement tunnel until they knew the extent of the invasion. Then the two men took Dog and disappeared immediately into the woods to search the area...and to find Brodwick.

One of the two men found Brodwick still out cold from a thrown rock. He'd known someone was around, he'd already alerted the other two, but he'd turned wrong. The others were already converging on their guests when the shot was fired. When a sweep of the area revealed no one else, Tanner and Laura took Brodwick to the local hospital in the Chevy station wagon. He had a concussion and would be kept there for several days.

Meanwhile at the hideaway, Daniels and Reed examined Rockwell's car and found a tracking device. That made the men look at each other. That's when they looked at Dog's flea collar. The bug was there.

On the way back from the hospital, Laura had the opportunity to ask, "Who was he?"

"George Rockwell," Tanner replied. "His uncle is a crook, and George Rockwell helped him. The uncle paid an impressive fine, but he didn't go to jail. Rockwell did."

Back at the cabin, the couple was shown Dog's collar and the bug. They'd all asked if the collar was new, but not if Tanner had bought it. They had to speculate quite a bit. Dog was attached to whoever it was who deliberately dropped him by the Moran beach house. It had not been Rockwell. The dog didn't know him. So someone else had been involved.

"How would they have known we would take Dog in?" Laura asked.

Daniels replied, "It was the only house around. When Dog got hungry enough, he'd have come to you. You would have fed him. Whoever dropped him there was hired by Rockwell to locate you and keep an eye on you until he could get there."

"Why would he think to bug the car? What made them think we might leave?"

"They were taking no chances. Under normal circumstances, the watchers would just keep track of you, but these guys who found you were pros and they were covering every possibility. With the change of cars, that tracking bug was lost, but there was still the chance you had Dog with you and the flea collar was still on him.

"Tracking is limited in range," he went on. "With you gone, they had to get within a reasonable distance to pick up the signal. So Rockwell had to cruise in a widening circle from Myrtle Beach in order to try to find the signal. And he found you. It was incredible that he did. That's what took him so long. If we had taken you farther, we might have thwarted him . . . for a while. He'd have found you eventually."

It was Laura who said, "The crook who hates not his crime, but the one who catches him." And the others agreed.

There was no charge brought against Tanner. There was no question it was self-defense. They were free to leave their haven.

It was rather strange to part from their three companions. A closeness had developed among them as happens when people share something unique. They had depended on each other, and by living in close quarters under such conditions they had come to know each other unusually well.

At the hospital Brodwick had said, "Don't say we'll be in touch, or send Christmas cards or anything. You can't prolong this kind of relationship. You two are good kids. Good luck to you."

Then as Laura and Tanner collected their various possessions, Daniels said the same thing. "We're glad the time is over for you, but forget it and get on with your lives. If you should ever need us again, we'll be there."

It was very strange.

But, of course, it wasn't over. It was only beginning. How does a woman convince a man that he is more important to her than her life? She and Tanner had changed roles. Now it was she who was committed and he was not. So how does a woman bring a man to commit himself? To know there is danger in just living?

She tried. "There are people who get killed by buses," she argued. "Tornadoes, lightning, stairs and unloaded guns. And there are a great number of people who never experience any danger at all and who finally die in bed, bored to death."

She talked all the way back as Tanner drove the borrowed car to the rendezvous with their stand-ins from the beach house and picked up the Porsche.

Laura was hardly distracted by the meeting. She thought the woman looked rather like her, but they'd missed matching Tanner altogether. No wonder Rockwell had ignored the decoys. As they drove off, Laura mentioned that to Tanner who had nothing to say.

They arrived at the beach house and it seemed years since they'd been there. It was dear and familiar, and she walked around and smiled at everything. Tanner was uncommunicative, busy as he replaced all the parts inside his computer and added the accoutrements to the phone. Dog wandered around seeing if anything had invaded his territory while he was gone, and he no longer watched the road.

"Tanner."

"Umm?"

"Will you marry me?"

"No."

"My mother will be shocked with me living in sin. I do hate to disappoint her. And then there's the in-

fluence on my younger sisters, and I have young female cousins that might also be influenced by such
conduct. I've always been a role model for them, so
you can see that you're probably wrecking another
whole generation of young Fullertons, and then there's
the Nance side of the family and those kids. They're
still a little young but kids are underestimated and they
are like walls, they have ears. And on the other side of
the family—''

"I'm not going to live with you either. We'll separate and go our own ways. I can't handle another time
like this."

"And I have nothing to say about it?" she chal-
lenged. "What about what I can handle? What if I
demand that you not drive another car because you
could get in the way of another idiot? How about if I
say you can never drive another car?"

"You know what I mean."

"I'll take your keys away and get your driver's license revoked."

He glanced at her, and when his eyes rested on her
a spark appeared in their depths. "How?"

She watched him stubbornly. "I'll find a way."

"Laura, you must understand."

"I can't. I only know you don't love me enough to
take any chances. I am willing to take whatever risks
are required. Rockwell was a fluke. He could have
been anything dangerous. He might have been a blue
racer, or a falling meteorite, or some fool's 'arrow shot
into the air.' If you don't love me enough to marry me

and take your chances, then you don't love me at all. You've had some pretty free sex lately, and you were very clever about it. I was under the mistaken impression that I meant something to you. I told you I'm not a bed hopper. The next man along the way will have a tough time breaking through the—"

"What next man?" he asked quietly.

"A brave one who will love me enough and be willing to take a chance on me."

"And I'm not brave enough?"

"Yes, you are. There's no going back. You love me. You need to realize how much. I need you. I want to share my life with yours. I love you very much."

"Oh, Laura, don't tempt me to risk you. I'd never be sure you were safe." He took her in his arms and held her tightly.

"I know, darling. This has all been very unusual." She moved away from him slightly and began to take off her clothes quite slowly. All's fair in love and war. This was both. She said kindly, "You need some normal time to balance out this past week. I can't guarantee you wouldn't have a dull life with me, but I'd try to keep you from being too bored." Quite seriously she discarded her panties and came to him, stark naked, standing against him and putting her arms around his shoulders and her hands into his hair holding his head sweetly.

"Laura, I do love you." He, too, was serious and his words were gentle.

She smiled, her eyes moist, and her fingers were moving in his hair. "I know you do."

"We have to separate."

"I think we should contribute our share to the horde of progeny who are privileged to visit this gorgeous old wreck of a house. Whose feet are causing the stairs to wear next to the banister, and whose hands are—"

"The stair treads are worn?"

"Quite noticeably...and whose laughter will be absorbed—"

"You're only making this harder."

"And whose fingers—"

"How many children?" It wasn't a question of curiosity, it was one of anguish.

"If I recall you're an only child. Only children tend to go overboard and have a veritable *horde* of children." She paused to consider then went on, "I would be willing to consider between four and six. I could tell you more after I see how difficult the first two are."

"Difficult?"

"I find you quite difficult to contend with. You are opinionated, obtuse and stubborn; and that's something for me to think about before I give you any terms."

"Explain this 'next man to come along.' You mentioned one a while ago and you haven't replied to my question." He frowned at her. "Do you have someone in mind?"

"Why is it when I take my clothes off and stand against you this way, I have your attention, but if I'm over there and dressed you don't want to marry me?"

His deep voice was emphatic. "If there was no danger to you, and you were encased in iron and I could never touch you, I'd want to be with you."

"That's a start."

"But, my love, if I kept you with me, you might be in danger. I cannot."

Her eyes studied him. He hadn't said, "can't" but "I cannot." The "cannot" was more serious. It was something insurmountable, which he'd studied and which he could not do. "Tanner, I love you more than my life."

"And I you. More than mine. I must let you go free. If I bind you to me, I put you at risk."

She leaned her forehead against his chest in despair, then she lifted her face to his and said, "Well, what will be, will be. Make love with me one last time."

His lips parted as he took in a sharp breath. "You're . . . leaving?"

"Yes. There's no purpose in staying."

"I . . . don't think I can let you go."

"What do you mean, you can't let me go? Make up your mind! I can't hang around waiting for crumbs."

"Is there another man?"

"No!" She was becoming impatient with him. "How could I have carried on with you this way if there was another man? Don't be ridiculous!"

His hands slid down the silk of her naked back and his fingers ran along her spine's dip at her waist. "Laura... It would be madness. I cannot. I must not. I can't risk you." His eyes were no longer filled with despair. They were focused on her in suffering.

"How boring."

"What?"

"You've said that forty times and I'm tired of hearing it!" She pushed away and began to pick up her clothes. She was deliberately slow, as she shook them out, and she turned with some knowledge of how she must look to him.

"Laura."

"It occurs to me that the only thing you want of me is sex. You could hardly wait to tumble me into bed after not seeing me in years. And I was so easy! It's rather annoying to admit that..." She frowned, her temper rising.

"Now..."

"So now the fun's over, and reality rears its head. All of the sudden I am 'at risk' and you dare not 'expose' me to danger. You're the danger, you rake! I came here—" She was a little hostile by then.

"You've got it all wrong."

"Do you want to marry me? Yes or no."

"Laura."

"A simple yes or no."

"No!" He was getting irritated with her. With some strained patience he began, "You have to understand...."

"I do. And I won't hound you, or beg or pester you. Goodbye. It's been fun." With her beautifully curved naked back to him, she began to dress.

Now it was he whose intentions turned around. He asked silkily, "How do you intend leaving? You have no car and I won't drive you."

"I'll call a cab." Over her shoulder she gave him a quick, enduring stare.

"The phone has been deactivated."

"Dog and I will hitchhike."

"No traffic."

"Then we'll walk."

Then he realized what she'd said, "*You* are taking Dog?"

"Yes. You can't have him. You might *jeopardize* him! Put him in harm's way." She glared.

"Laura..."

"Goodbye, Tanner."

Pulling her middie blouse down over her head, she stormed toward the front door in a temper. She arrived just as a knock sounded. Very irritated, Laura jerked the door open with one hand, just as she pulled her blouse down over her body with her other hand. Henry, the vet, was somewhat startled.

Her face was red and angry, and she snapped, "Henry, would you take me into Myrtle Beach to the airport? I need to go there and Tanner refuses to drive me."

Henry cautiously looked over at Tanner who was about as placid as a storm looming on the horizon. So Henry said tentatively, "Well . . ."

"I'll pay for your trouble." She was furious with Tanner by then and edging into being hateful to poor Henry.

"No, no, no. Uh. Tanner?"

She tattled to Henry. "He disabled the phone too."

"I gotta be going." Henry tried backing out of the situation. "Listen to Tanner. He'll figure things out."

"Henry—" she was killingly calm "—if you don't take me into Myrtle Beach, I'll have to hitchhike."

Any veterinarian has a soft heart. Everyone *knows* a veterinarian is a pushover for anything in distress. Henry said, "Tanner, I'm going to do it. If you can't solve whatever it is, right now, I'm going to take her into town."

Tanner didn't say anything. His stormy eyes never left Laura, but he didn't interfere.

She went up the stairs to her room. Her "double" had left the room spotless and put fresh sheets on the bed. Laura pulled her clothes off and fought her tears. She dressed in one of her two suits, with panty hose and heels. She took her other things from their hangers, scooped up her shoes and threw her clothes into her bag, then she gathered the closet clothes she had worn and put them in a heap. She hesitated when she saw the red dress. It would only remind her of Tanner. She'd just leave it there, and she added it to the pile of clothes to be washed.

It was Henry who met her on the stairs and took her bag and carried it out to the car. She went back to her room for the bundle of clothes she'd worn and carried it down, through the kitchen, to the laundry room to put it into the washer, add soap and start the load washing.

"You haven't had lunch."

She looked up at Tanner but only very briefly. If she really looked at him she would cry. "I'm not hungry."

"Don't leave this way."

"How then? What would you suggest? A hot-air balloon?"

"Don't be angry with me."

"I'm not. It's just that I've never been able to endure deliberate idiots."

"Laura, you're killing me." His voice cracked.

Her heart was about to break in two. "The closet clothes will be washed; sorry not to get them dried and folded."

"Laura..."

She went on out into the big center hall, where Henry stood waiting. She looked toward the morning room, holding its supply of perfect equipment, where she could have been content to work for the rest of her life, but she couldn't bear to go in for a final look around.

She had her own case of supplies, the things she'd left home with, plus the sketches she'd done at the beach cottage, and those she'd done of Tanner at the hideaway. She had no excuse not to leave. But she stood there.

Henry cautioned Laura with gentleness, "You must not take Dog. He's gotten used to you two. To throw him into a carrier and drag him off in a plane would be cruel...."

Tanner came from the kitchen as Laura said, "I know." She looked at Dog who was alert and curious. The human emotions were running high. He couldn't figure it out at all. In her guest voice, Laura said, "Thank you, Tanner, for an interesting and... different two weeks. It's been unusual."

Ignoring an appalled Henry who didn't know what on earth to do to help these creatures, Tanner said to Laura, "Kiss me goodbye."

She couldn't see him through her tears. "I can't." There was no concealing how her voice wavered. She'd come apart if she kissed him. He probably knew that.

Very gently, Henry said, "Come along." Carrying her bag, he held the screen door for her, and she went out onto the porch.

Tanner asked her, "Do you have enough money?"

She didn't look back, she was trying to see the steps as she went down them. She mumbled a strangled, "Yes."

But then Dog went down the steps and tagged along to Henry's car. He didn't go close to it, but stopped to watch as the car door was opened and it was apparent she was going to get into that car. He made an inquiring sound in his throat that wasn't a whine or a bark.

Laura exchanged a long look with Dog and then she bent down and hugged him. He held still for it. She then got quickly into the car. Henry went around and got in to his side, started it and they backed from the drive, turned and went off down the road, leaving Tanner and the dog watching after them.

She cried all the way to the airport, and Henry didn't say a word. He found it was a lot easier to deal with animals than with people. You could pet an animal and talk to it and not have to pick and choose words or understand anything but its physical pain. People were another whole mess.

Piedmont Airline had a plane that left in the middle of the afternoon, flying to Dayton and then going on to South Bend. Laura told Henry goodbye and asked him not to stay because she wasn't good company. He agreed absentmindedly. He stood around for a while and, about the third time she told him thank you and goodbye, he shook his head and said, "You didn't seem to be such a quitter." Then he left her sitting there with her mouth open in huffy indignation.

He went back to Tanner. Along with Dog he sat around with the silent Tanner. Finally he said, "If you truly love someone, then you fight for her."

Ten

────

Having arrived at the airport far too early for the Piedmont flight, Laura had more than sufficient time to think about Henry's accusation. A quitter? She had never in her entire life been labeled a quitter. Was she? Had she given up too soon?

Was it Ann Landers who said, "In order to judge a relationship with anyone, you have to decide whether you are better off with or without that person"?

Tanner's face came strongly into Laura's mind and she had the leisure to contemplate all his expressions. His thoughtfulness, his humor, his appreciation of her. His eyes dancing in amused interest, the flames of his passion burning there.

Laura sat in the airport, thinking about Tanner. If he didn't want her, why had he asked her to stay with him? Why had he trapped her heart forever? Her love, her own desire. Actually he'd claimed her all those years ago with that first kiss, there at Indiana University by the Jordan River. She would have gone with him that day, lived with him and been his love, but he'd walked on off as if her presence hadn't really registered with him.

Tanner did desire her. She hadn't needed to make that red dress for his seduction, and she smiled as she remembered Tanner's hilarious responses to her requirements for his conduct. He was so marvelously humorous. And she remembered how he'd loved her. How he'd not been able to keep his hands from her, his face flushed with his desire, his eyes hot, his smile so wickedly delighted with her. How could he have done all that if he didn't want her?

Was she better off without him? No. She'd always yearned for Tanner Moran. Tanner hadn't lured her into his volcanic lair. She'd gone there wanting him. How could she leave him? Not without a better try. All her pioneer ancestors would be embarrassed by her meekly leaving without at least a more concerted effort. She wanted to be with him. She found her mind was repeating his name endlessly. She had never forgotten him. She never would.

Laura opened her sketchbook and looked at the drawings she had made of Tanner at the beach house. They were all she had of him. And she contrasted the lazy, humorous Tanner she'd drawn at the beach house to the tense Tanner at the hideaway.

As willing as she was to flaunt any danger, when it was balanced against being with Tanner, could she put him through the worry of danger to her? Not to consider his concern would be selfish of her. She worried over that with as much fairness as she could. She decided—equally as fairly—that if they were ever to be together, as fate intended they should be, then it would have to be by his choice. It was something he would have to work out for himself, however. It wouldn't be unfair of her to be around while he decided, but only to remind him she existed.

She had no problem throwing fate into the middle of her fair-unfair argument. Any fool's subconscious knows when to nudge the balance. With fate allowed into the argument, her sense of having been misused strengthened, and a healing irritation began to grow in her. She felt he'd underestimated her. She was a strong, mature woman. She could handle whatever came her way. Anyone can live a completely risk-free life in bed—alone, naturally. Of course the house might catch on fire and the decision would have to be made to leave the bed. No one lived without some risk.

How could she go back now, after she'd flung out of his house that way? How could she act, under such circumstances, so that she didn't look foolish? She could go back to the Moran cottage and say, "Oh, hi. I was just passing by. . . ." Or she could be honest and tell him, "I'm here for as long as you'll let me stay.

Until you ask me to leave again.'' That's what she'd do.

She had taken so long, in her remembering and deciding, that it was almost flight time when she returned her ticket, retrieved her luggage and snared a cab.

As the cab drove north from Myrtle Beach, a Porsche went by them, going south on the lonely road. Was it Tanner? After the brief glimpse, she didn't look again. How could she chase him in a cab? Was he, too, leaving the Moran cottage? What if she got out there and he was gone? He could have put all his computer parts in a basket, gathered his things and left. What would she do out there if he'd gone? No phone, no transportation. She'd have to break into the house. What was she doing going recklessly back to Tanner?

Dog was sitting on the porch and he smiled at her when she emerged from the cab. But Tanner could have left Dog there, with a call to Henry to pick the animal up. Tanner had suggested doing that when they'd gone to the hideout. She said to the cab driver, "Would you wait just a minute?" He turned off his motor.

The front door wasn't locked. She went inside to Tanner's study, and on the desk the computer and all its parts were still there. Tanner was coming back. She went out, paid the driver, took her luggage and watched the cab drive away. Her last link with sanity.

She straightened up bracingly, breathed deeply and marched up onto the porch, her heels sounding on the wooden steps. She vividly recalled the first time she walked up those steps to that porch with Pete's bouquet in her hand as an excuse to see Tanner again. She went inside, and everything was so dearly familiar. Some qualms caused her to shiver. Was she right in doing this?

She put her suitcase down in the center hall and slowly walked in a circle with her hands comfortingly holding her face, then she took another deep breath and went up to her room. There she efficiently unpacked.

She went down to take the load of clothes from the washer, to put them into the dryer so that she would have something to wear. But the clothes were out on the kitchen table and neatly folded. She thought of Tanner's hands folding the clothes she'd worn, and she wondered what his thoughts had been.

As she carried the clothes up to her room, she considered what she should wear. Not the red dress. Sex wasn't all there was to a relationship. She should be dressed in a fairly normal way. Like a reasonable, mature woman. The party girl/sexpot wasn't companion material. In her room, she put the cleaned clothes in various drawers, and the red dress was nowhere to be found. It was such wispy, asinine material it was either stuck in the drain of the washer or had disintegrated in the dryer. Lousy material but . . . very effective. There is a time and place for red dresses.

This, however, was not a red dress time. Then why was she becoming distractedly irritated in not finding it?

She put on the dark blue and light green wraparound and the thongs. She let her hair free and brushed it as she looked at herself in the mirror. Then she very, very carefully put on makeup, rejected using some of the mismatched earrings in the cigar box of costume jewelry, and went downstairs to the kitchen to sort through the freezer. She made her choice, shunning an apple pie that looked as if Pam had made it, and paced slowly around. Out on the front porch she spoke to Dog, then decided it wouldn't look right for her to be waiting on the front porch for Tanner to come back. She was going to be aloof, logical and patiently mature. Pretty soon now.

It *had* been Tanner's Porsche that had passed the cab, and he'd noted the cab, oddly that far north of town, and the shadow in the back seat had been...feminine? But flight time was looming and he had to catch Laura before she left. He couldn't risk following a cab with a shadow woman in the back seat. What if it hadn't been Laura?

So he did go to the airport, and he did find she'd canceled at the last minute, and he did drive back to the cottage rather pressingly. He saw no difference in the house to tell him if she was there. He drove into the garage and, feeling stretched by his emotions, he went up the back steps to the deck and flung open the screen to enter the kitchen.

She was there. He stood, looking at her. She gave him a cool glance and went on with her preparations for dinner. He moved to her with an anguished, "Laura..." and she stepped neatly aside. She didn't say anything.

She'd had all those neat things to say, so coolly and maturely, but she found she was very annoyed he was actually safely back... and there. She didn't really intend her lack of warm response as punishment for her own tears, but she was rather surprisingly angry with him.

And since he was meltingly loving to find her there, her coolness puzzled him. He stood there, watching her with tender eyes. With a needless busyness, she walked around him, with pointed impatience that indicated he was in her way. He said in a throaty purr, "You came back."

One is not always in control of one's tongue. Quite coldly she replied, "I believe I missed the name?"

He looked surprised, then he said warningly, "Laura..."

"Well, if you know mine, I should indeed know yours, give me a hint." She was very prickly.

He was, too. "A hint? You asked me to marry you not too long ago."

"Oh," she said dismissively. "One of those." She turned away very efficiently and continued her preparations.

He was at a loss. He had no idea why she should be angry with him. But she *was* there. He stood in the middle of the room, watching her, trying to find a way to talk to her; and she finally told him, "Move."

He went over by the door to the dining room and stood there, then he leaned against the jamb, as finally he just relaxed and watched her. She was really mad at him. Why? She moved so beautifully. Her color was a little heightened. Her body was just inside that handy wraparound. What would it take to placate her?

In silence they sat down to eat, and she had no real idea what she'd served, or if it was edible food, or even how it tasted. She was well aware that she could not continue this ridiculous behavior, and her color was high because she had embarrassed herself by being so silly. Mature and in command was the only way to behave. She was girding up to speak when he said softly, "I'm here, Laura, look at me."

She blurted, "I'm not speaking to you."

"Why?" It was a reasonable question.

"Because I'm mad that you would discard me so readily. You didn't give me any say in anything."

"Honey—"

"For me to leave was only pandering to your idiosyncrasies."

He straightened up and inquired, "My... idiosyncrasies? Being concerned for your safety is hardly in the category of idiosyncrasy, Laura, you—"

"I'm not through. I believe we should have some time as just friends." She watched him laugh, then said sternly, "Just because I'm furious with you that's no call for you to laugh. I may not be speaking to you, but I believe I need to explain why I'm here."

"I don't care *why* you're here, so long as you are."

She ignored that and continued, "We've had a week of sex and a week of danger. This isn't anything like most people have, and our emotions are very unreliable. I believe we need some time to have an ordinary, friendship relationship. No sex. Just a courteous time with ordinary conversation. Learning about each other." Her words weren't as smooth or reasonable as she wanted them to be. He distracted her from what she was saying. He did that by giving her his entire attention, which was well enough, but his eyes were so amused and the flames were obvious. He wasn't accepting her premise. He was indulging her. How like a man with a woman.

She told him primly, "I'm in love with you. No, sit still. I want you to listen to me. I'm not sure if I'm truly in love or if I'm mesmerized by the idea of you. I've always been unreasonable in my reaction to you. I really came here to exorcise you from my dreams. Tanner, if you don't sit still and listen to me I'm going to leave here. I'm much too susceptible to you. We could go right to bed and I would never know if I stayed here because I really love you or if I just wanted you."

He smiled and leaned back in his chair. "There isn't any question at all, Laura. It's like that with both of us."

"I'm from pioneer stock. The women in my family coped with men who had to see what was over the next hill, who settled in dangerous places, where there were unwelcoming Indians, cholera, saddle tramps, isolation and hard work. I'm no ninny. I can cope. I need to know if what I feel for you is true."

"Oh, my love."

"Don't get mushy. This is serious. Pretty soon all your nieces and nephews will be here, and you'll have to think of something to explain me. They'll know I have no honorable business here. They'll point at you and scrape the opposite forefinger along the pointing one in a shaming sign. I'd be ashamed."

"Don't you trust me?"

"The government might, but I'm not sure I should. While I do love you, right now I don't much like you. I can't understand why you made me leave."

"But you came back to me." He smiled that Tanner Moran smile of his.

She looked away from him before she could reply soberly, "You never took me sailing."

That confused him and he inquired, "Sailing?"

"When I first came here, you asked me if I sailed and when I said I was a prairie woman, you said I needed to try sailing. You could do that while we're being friends. Can you behave for a week and be friends?"

"How about friendly friends?"

"It won't work, Tanner. We need time to know each other."

"I know all that needs knowing about you. Haven't you learned anything about me?"

"I know you're more complicated than I thought. There are depths to you I hadn't known about. I saw you move like a shadow, so fast, and you attacked that man. I hadn't realized you could do something like that."

"At all costs, I had to protect you."

"He didn't want me; he was after you."

"I was surprised he didn't shoot from ambush. It's ambush that scares the hell out of me. I was almost sick with worry that you would be hurt."

"In Fort Wayne, Indiana, the Children's Zoo has an alligator in the moat around the monkey island." Tanner looked a little blank, so she explained, "The alligator was put there to add stress so the monkeys don't get bored. Life without some stress is too dull. So to be healthy, you need some problems. I'm glad you got Rockwell."

"I believe the killing was an accident. When I saw Rockwell come from behind that tree with a gun, I thought only to stop him. I'm not completely sure that Dog's simultaneous attack threw me off that much. I'm not sure I didn't mean to kill him. That's a tough question for a civilized man to have to live with. Rockwell did have other problems. We're finding out more about him. He wasn't balanced or he'd never have come after me. Any criminal who blames the catcher isn't working with a full deck. He had a gun. I knew how to handle that. But I hadn't expected Dog to feel such loyalty so soon. I hadn't realized Dog meant to help.''

"I was no help at all.''

"I'm only grateful you didn't try. You did exactly right. You did nothing to attract his attention to you, and I could keep it on me.''

"I was terrified.''

"We are, too, when we're in danger, but we've been taught to use the adrenaline to help ourselves. It's the same channeling of emotion used by fighters before a big bout, or by actors who have stage fright. We'd be stupid to say we're not afraid. We simply use the fear productively in our own protection. In all this there was only one loose end. We needed to know who had found me and why they'd helped Rockwell. It was they who'd dropped Dog and bugged his collar and the Porsche.

"We found the finders are professional investigators. They're ordinary businessmen. They're very good at their job. They're busy and had no trouble believing finding me was quite routine, search and find. They'll be more careful after this. Do a little more thorough checking on their client.'' He looked at her very seriously. "Laura, I can never let you go free again.''

"I never wanted to be free of you. You're the one who was dead set against my staying with you. Why have you changed your mind?''

"I almost missed getting you off that plane, had you been on it, because I really put the pressure on the organization to finish the scan. To find if there could possibly be another, potential Rockwell. There is no one. Life from here on out should be quite routine and very dull. You have to save me. That's why I went after you. But you were here.'' It was important to him that she'd returned on her own.

"Save you?" She frowned at him. "Save you from what?"

"Boredom. A loveless life. Loneliness. Be the alligator in my moat. I love you with all my heart and soul. Marry me, Laura."

"Your...alligator?" She stared. Then she whispered, "I'll think about it." And her eyes were enormous.

"You know you have nothing to be afraid of with me."

"No?" She moved a little, lifting her chin, again in touch with her situation. Rather saucily, she asked, "How many times have you pulled this caper? Seducing and then relinquishing a woman for *her own* safety? You're really a scoundrel."

His smile was slow and very dangerous. "I? I was here all alone, unable to walk well, and you came along and seduced me."

"That isn't true. You could too walk! You sneak! You deliberately fooled me with that crutch."

He went on smiling that smug, naughty smile. "If I recall correctly, it was you who made a red dress to catch my fancy."

"You did too seduce me. You lugged me across the floor over your hip and displaced my whole rib cage. I had to have my whole chassis realigned."

"Really?" He rose from his chair at the table. "Let me see."

She stood up and backed toward the center hall. "You're to keep your distance," she warned, holding one hand out to warn off his advance.

It is a rash woman who pushes a man too far. She had. His long swift stride closed the space between them. His arms went around her, enclosing her closely, so close her breasts were squashed against his hard chest and her arms flew out. Then he kissed her.

Her head felt as if it floated off. Of course it couldn't actually, he was holding it with one big hand so she couldn't move from his kiss, but it still felt that way. Her whole body seemed unorganized, swamped with sensation and a little out of control. It was as if she ought to hold on to something in order not to become too disoriented. He was handy, being there so close to her, so she held on to him.

She should resist. This was to be friendship week. No hanky-panky. He was pulling this same thing again. He was going to seduce her. She should resist. She wasn't a pushover. He was kissing her unfairly with the Tanner Talent that drove women wild. He was doing that to her. She should ... His mouth was marvelous. How could he be so gentle and so masterful and so sensual at the same time?

Her body relaxed, aware how lovely it was to be against Tanner. To have his hard arms around her and to feel him close, to hear his unsteady breath, the sounds in his throat, to feel his heart thundering....

His hands moved along, on, over and cupped. So strong, so nice, so... She really ought to...what should she "ought" to do? Kiss back? That had to be the feeling urgently trying to communicate to her. That she should do...what? She couldn't figure anything else she wanted to do, so she kissed him back quite willingly.

Her fingers worked their way through his hair in slow, sensuous combings. Her body squirmed a bit and trembled with desire, and her breath gasped. Her knees bent and pushed her hips against his, and he made pleasured sounds.

She really...what? She really was glad he was there. When he lifted his mouth from hers, or actually he only slid it from hers to kiss along her cheek in greedy nibblings, she was surprised as she said in a gasp, "Where is my red dress?"

He laughed; a low, deliciously wicked chuckle that rumbled in his chest. "Don't forget, it's mine. You made it for me."

"That's silly! What would you do with it? It's mine!"

"I *would* let you wear it for me."

She hadn't meant that, not now, maybe next week. She said, "I couldn't find it. If it went into the guest closet, it could well shock someone." She lay back in his arms, her fingers still at the back of his head and she looked up at him. Her heart turned over and she couldn't remember what they'd been talking about, he was so dear. She loved him so much. She might have lost him. But he was there, holding her.

"It's in my inside jacket pocket. But it's mine."

The dress, he was talking about the dress. "It wouldn't fit in there. Let me see."

"Only if you intend to put it on."

"No." Her lips said the word very slowly and her lashes drooped by themselves.

He said with soft urgency, "I have to make love to you."

She shook her head so minimally that it could be ignored. He released her and moved back a step as her hands trailed off his shoulders as if they'd been abandoned. She frowned as her lips parted to take in a breath to protest his leaving her, but she forgot to voice her protest because he just stood there and looked at her.

His eyes looked down at her hotly, and then he smiled that Tanner way, as he reached into the pocket and pulled out a thin streak of red, just as a magician might do, and the streak floated out and became a limp garment. She'd worn *that*? How shocking!

He looked at her as he shrugged out of his jacket and began to unbutton his shirt.

"Oh, no you don't," she cautioned.

He pulled off the shirt and tossed aside shoes and socks. then, in front of her captive eyes, he unbuckled his trousers and slid them off his hips and kicked them aside. He watched her as he discarded his briefs and stood there before her.

It wasn't only because she was an artist that her eyes consumed him. He was so marvelously male. The streaks of healing scars only enhanced his pirate image. He could make a *fortune* for *Playgirl*. She'd break his neck if he did. She had to paint him. What was she thinking?

He came to her, and she didn't turn away, or run, or even take a backward step. She opened her arms to him. He undid and opened the wraparound dress. She didn't say one word of protest. He peeled the shoulders down her arms, and she moved them to help him. He took her panties off, as easily, and they joined the growing pile of discarded clothing. His eyelashes moved down over his eyes as he looked at her, then his relishing hands began.

"Tanner..."

"Well, how about that? You do remember my name!" He picked up the red dress and pulled the flimsy, wicked thing down over her head, then he tousled her sun-streaked hair into a careless, wanton mass. With narrowed, smiling, passion-flamed eyes, he said, "There you are." And he began to touch her through the fragile silk. He groaned and held her to him. "Put your hands on me."

"Oh, Tanner, what are you doing to me?"

"I'm going to make love to you for the rest of our lives. You need to marry me so the nieces and nephews won't be shocked."

"Marry you?" She acted as if that was the first time marriage had been mentioned.

His eyes were deadly serious as he looked down at her. "Yes."

"Oh, Tanner..." He really made her a little unsettled. "This is our friendship week." That was an odd thing to say when she was plastered there against his naked body.

"I like being friendly with you."

"Well..." she began. She looked up at him, and he was so confident.

He acted as if that had been the reply he wanted to hear as he said, "Me too. I do have to know how many kids we're going to have, so I can build a house that's big enough." Then he kissed her in such a lovely way, hugging her tightly in that red silken dress. His eyes were brimming with amusement and the flaming coals of his passion. He lifted her and carried her to his bed, only limping somewhat. He laid her on his bed and followed her quite easily.

The bed was soft and sensuously welcoming, enfolding them. By degrees he removed the red silk that covered her so seductively, so invitingly. And he made love to her.

Laura helped. She made it easy for him, in that first of their friendship week. Helping was a little embarrassing under her blatant disregard of her rules, and she blushed a little. She turned for him as he relished her and her breath became a little ragged. Soon she squeaked and wiggled and moaned as she twitched, and the fires of desire flamed high and hot in both of them. She felt abandoned and quite reckless.

He nibbled and kissed and suckled as their skins filmed from their labors causing them to slither as they rubbed together, enjoying the differences of their bodies. Their mouths were eager and demanding, their hearts racing with their thrills as they loved each other. She cried out with her need and he took her with care, then they rode the glory trail with exquisite movement, delaying, hesitating, writhing and finally flying off into ecstasy.

As she lay dormant, he trembled still, his kisses softened, his hands gentled. He moved minutely, no longer desperate. He sighed and his words were sweet. "I love you. You're my own. My dream. My love."

And she heard herself: "You're here. You're *here*! You're real. Oh, Tanner. I love you, too. Marry me."

"How soon?"

"Soon. Very soon."

He stayed with her as he kissed her, propped on his elbows, his fingers playing with her hair as he talked to her, petting her, and eventually he again made love to her. She laughed then, and wiggled and teased. And so did he, but he had his way with her, and then—like their bodies—their lives came together just as fate had intended all along.

Silhouette Desire

**Available
January 1987**

NEVADA
SILVER

The third book in the exciting
Desire Trilogy by Joan Hohl.

The Sharp brothers are back, along with
sister Kit ... and Logan McKittrick.

Kit's loved Logan all her life and, with a little
help from the silver glow of a Nevada night,
she must convince the stubborn rancher that
she's a woman who needs a man's love—not
the protection of another brother.

Don't miss *Nevada Silver*—Kit and
Logan's story and the conclusion
of Joan Hohl's acclaimed
Desire Trilogy.